Pressure to Mutilate

MATTHEW UZUKWU

SCRIPTOR HOUSE
THE EPITOME OF GREATNESS

Dedication

For Stephanie and Chinwe.

Copyright © 2022 by Matthew Uzukwu.

Matthew Uzukwu is on Twitter, Instagram and Facebook.

Paperback ISBN: 979-8-88692-038-3
Ebook Epub ISBN: 979-8-88692-039-0

"...Mama, I want to announce to you that my wife gave birth to a bouncing baby girl."

"Congratulations, my son! The same goes to your wife!"

"Thank you, mama."

"Since she is a girl, I hope you will do what our culture demands of you to do," said Bilky.

"What is that, mama?"

"Her circumcision," Bilky replied.

Osak was quiet for a couple of minutes, at a loss of what to say to his mother.

"Are you still there?" she inquired, thinking he had hung up.

"Mama, I am still here."

"Did you hear what I said?"

"I did mama, but I'm not sure my wife will agree with that. Remember she is white, and they do not have this kind of practice in their culture."

"Osak, do not forget your cultural heritage," scolded Bilky.

CHAPTER 1

Ingrid was in labor for several hours. Her pregnancy had been a difficult one. After experiencing three miscarriages, this pregnancy, for which she had lain in bed for several hours waiting to deliver the baby, had stuck. Osak, her ebony skinned husband of 4 years, mustachioed, tall and handsome, paced up and down Ingrid's room in the hospital. He was nervous at the frenetic activity involving nurses, doctors and others who were present to attend to his wife. His white shirt was rumpled from lying on a recliner in the corner of the room where he had been keeping vigil as Ingrid went through her labor pains. Ingrid received medication to numb the excruciating pain she felt as she prepared to deliver her first child. Her doctors decided at some point that a natural birth posed a risk to both her and her child, and a decision was made to carry out a C-section. Ingrid was put to sleep and the doctors went to work. About an hour or so later, she delivered a healthy baby girl. The baby cried loudly as she took her first breaths.

"Oh, she is a feisty one," said one of the nurses in jest. She held her delicately and started to clean her up.

Ingrid was all smiles as she looked at the baby. Osak walked up close and kissed her. He beamed as well, showing impeccable white teeth. This attribute, Ingrid had once told him, was one of several in him that attracted him to her. Ingrid did not tell him that 'white teeth' was a stereotype she had of Africans. Her father had once told her that Africans were too poor to indulge in expensive food and drinks which were loaded with multiple coloring and additives to give them yellow teeth as was the case in America, where fast food joints clogged every block of every city. By coincidence, Ingrid's keen interest in watching documentaries of Africa, and her chance meeting with a few Africans in college seemed to confirm her dad's observation. The smiles in those documentaries and of those African college students she had met were always white.

"Congratulations, my dear wife?" said a still

smiling and very happy Osak.

Ingrid beamed as well. "Thank you! What are we gonna name her?"

"I will let you choose the name," said Osak.

"My grandmother was named Felicia. It's a lovely name. I knew her as a child and she was one of my favorite people. I will name her after my grandmother."

"That's great," said Osak. "I think it's a nice name."

Ingrid was discharged after a one week stay at the hospital. The cesarean nature of her birthing had required close monitoring for a few days by her doctors. Her history with difficult pregnancy had to be taken into consideration as well. On her going home day, Osak had pulled up his Toyota Highlander to the entrance of the Washington Hospital Center at about 12 noon to pick her and their baby daughter up. The vehicle was festooned with balloons and flowers to capture and revere in the glorious moment.

Osak drove carefully and he attracted not a few eyes to his vehicle which stood out with all the decorations on it. After driving through the lunch hour traffic of northeast Washington DC and suburban Maryland for about an hour, they arrived at their single family home on a cul-de-sac in a leafy estate. Osak pulled into the garage then assisted Ingrid, who still ached, into the family room through an adjoining door. Felicia was wrapped up in blankets. She had been born on a snowy January winter morning. Her pink face looked adorable, and she had a smile on her face.

Safely inside the house now, and having made sure that Ingrid was comfortable in bed, with Felicia next to her, Osak went downstairs to the basement to his office to make a call to his parents, who lived in Africa, to break the good news to them. He first called his father but could not get through to him. He next called his mother who picked up after a few rings of the phone. Bilky, Osak's mother, was a brown skinned woman of average build and height who stood at 5 feet and 6 inches tall.

"Hello mother." Osak greeted.

"Hello son, how are you?"

"I am well. I hope you are too!"

"Yes, we are. Your dad and sister are all very fine."

"That's very good. I have good news for you," teased Osak.

"What is it?"

"I want to announce to you that my wife gave birth to a bouncing baby girl."

"Congratulations, my son! The same goes to your wife!"

"Thank you, mama."

"Since she is a girl, I hope you will do what our culture demands of you to do," said Bilky.

"What is that, mama?"

"Her circumcision," Bilky replied.

Osak was quiet for a couple of minutes, at a loss of what to say to his mother.

"Are you still there?" she inquired, thinking he had hung up.

"Mama, I am still here."

"Did you hear what I said?"

"I did mama, but I'm not sure my wife will agree with that. Remember she is white, and they do not have this kind of practice in their culture."

"Osak, do not forget your cultural heritage," scolded Bilky. "When you first told us you wanted to marry this white woman, I warned you not to do it. I suspected issues like this would come up, but you said you were in love and couldn't live without her. Now, see the situation you have found yourself in. You can't do what culture demands of you because of your wife. Osak, it's pathetic!"

"Mama, I made my choice. This circumcision you talk about is old fashioned. Nobody does that anymore, even in our country."

"Osak, you are from a royal family which is bound to adhere to all cultural practices as custodians of our community's ancient culture. That others are doing different things today do not mean we must do as they are doing. Our family neglects upholding our culture at our peril, including mysterious deaths. Supernatural forces could take your life over it."

"Ok mama, I will think about it and get back to you."

"You must make up your mind quickly. We can do the circumcision here. It doesn't have to be done in America."

Osak got off the phone and immediately went into a depressive state from the conversation he had just had with his mother. His mind filled up quickly with riotous thoughts about everything—his traditionalist family back home, his new life in America, and the balance he must strike between the modern influences in his life and the anachronistic beliefs and practices of his place of origin.

Osak was raised a Muslim but converted to Christianity during secondary school, which he had attended at a private Christian academy. King Ebu, Osak's father, was the traditional ruler of a community of 50,000 people. He was burly, charcoal black and very tall. Osak was thus a prince. Growing up in the palace of his father, he had witnessed from close quarters various practices associated with his father's position as king. Culture required of his father to be polygamous. Thus his dad had married five wives. Osak's mother was the first wife. King Ebu graced all traditional festivals where he presided over religious rituals and animal sacrifices. As heir to the throne, Osak was compelled to be around King Ebu a lot to learn about the duties of a king, and the methods of cultural and ritual practice. King Ebu was also a semi modern man who believed in the benefits of modern society and its components, especially education. Osak had entered secondary school and became exposed to Western cultural influences. He became enamored with American R & B music and American films. He became a voracious consumer of stories about America, its icons, people, arts and culture. He could enter any university of his choice in the country, upon completion of secondary school, by virtue of his brilliance and royal connections, but he made up his mind to seek higher education in the USA. King Ebu had wanted his son to further his education in the country, for fear he would be softened up by Western culture and be compelled to turn his back on his community. But Osak had convinced his father he would maintain fidelity to the community and its culture and traditions. That fidelity was now put to the test in the conversation he had just had with his mother.

Osak's heart raced as he sat in his chair surfing the internet, his mind not particularly on the displays shown on the computer screen. The riotous thoughts which had attacked his mind were now subsiding, but not before another bout which took him down memory lane about how he had met Ingrid and how their relationship had blossomed into marriage. It had been 5 years now since that encounter in a nightclub, located just off campus at the college he and Ingrid attended.

He was an Accounting Junior while she was a sophomore studying Political Science as a stepping stone to Law School. They crossed paths every now and then in dining halls, at college football games as spectators, and in the school library.

They said nothing to each other. Ingrid was probably not thinking about him, but Osak was infatuated with her. Ingrid was white quite alright, but Osak's infatuation with her emanated mostly from her physical attributes. Growing up in Africa, Osak's stereotypical white woman preferred by white men was the slim, almost thin and gangly kind. He had seen clips of boardwalks, and all the models fit into this physical characteristic. But Ingrid was somewhat thick, without being fat, with a handsome backside, the kind of physique favored by African men, and there weren't that many women on the overwhelmingly white college campus with that kind of physique. He had to have her as a friend, he vowed, but he was shy and was unsure of what Ingrid's reaction would be if he made a move. He had never dated a white girl before. He recalled the admonition he received from his father on the eve of his departure for the USA not to marry a white woman, or any other woman for that matter who lived in America. His wife must be someone from the community back home. Osak's father even intimated him about an arrangement he had already made for Osak to marry a woman from the community upon the completion of his education and return home to the country.

King Ebu's plans were relegated to the far recesses of Osak's mind, which at this point was focused on how he could win the love of this young woman who had mesmerized him so much. A fateful encounter occurred in a night club one summer night. The club's patronage was halved as a consequence of the summer break and most students taking off for home. The few students who had remained on campus were either taking classes or were employed at summer jobs in and around campus. Ingrid was taking a summer class while Osak worked a summer job at a nearby bakery.

Ingrid was about 5 feet 9 inches tall, nicely oblong faced, and blonde haired. She was busty and curvaceous. Osak's captivation was understandable in this context. Ingrid had strolled into the club with a friend of hers at about 8pm when heavy clubbing activity was about to start. Osak, who had clocked off work about an hour earlier, sat in a corner of the club. It was a Saturday night, a day of the week he typically set aside for fun activity after pulling an 80-hour work week in a grueling summer work schedule to save up money for the coming fall semester. He sipped coca cola from a tall glass. Soft music played in the background, as the DJ prepared to steer the night in a louder direction.

Soon the DJ's signature callout that things were about to get funky, rent the air—a howl which mimicked a coyote's, pumped up exhortations, and a loud base from large speakers.

"Come on now, get your asses off of your damned chairs and get busy on the damned floor," he yelled to hoots and whistles from the excited young college crowd. They responded to his energy and flooded the dance floor to a loud R&B number.

Ingrid was among the raiders of the dance floor. They jumped and gyrated to a song aptly named RAID by the Lakeside R&B Band. Osak eyed the dance floor of young revelers. They were overwhelmingly white. He was among a sprinkling of blacks in the night club crowd. Long ago, when he had arrived on his first day of school, he felt intimidated and out of place on the almost lily white campus. But in the course of three years and to his surprise, he never experienced any overt acts of racial discrimination. He had instinctively gravitated to black students on campus, particularly those from Africa, like him, but he also had a smattering of white male friends, never a white girlfriend, though. Ingrid was therefore the first major move he contemplated making to date interracially.

Osak was shy, but when started up like a rocket, he could hold a conversation pretty decently. He stared at Ingrid, who danced away on the dance floor, oblivious to the looks of rapture from the young African guy sitting several steps away from the dance floor, sipping a soft drink. Then the music stopped after what had seemed an eternity, for the dancers to catch a breather. Ingrid and her friend walked off the dance floor to their table, set several steps away from where Osak sat. This was Osak's moment to make his move. He took a final sip of his drink and stood up. He walked leisurely over to where Ingrid sat with her friend and introduced himself.

"Hello pretty ladies, I am Osak, may I sit with you?"

Ingrid and her friend stared at each other. The sudden intrusion was a bit uncomfortable for them, but Ingrid recovered quicker than her friend.

"Sure!" she answered. "Jen, do you mind?" she asked her friend.

"No!" said Jen.

There was an awkward silence for a couple minutes until Osak broke the ice, self deprecatingly.

"Ladies, you can call me a rude gnat for the way I barged into your space like that, but I come in peace."

"Who are you again?" asked Ingrid.

"Osak, an African and a very special man."

The women laughed

"Why are you special?" Jen asked.

"I once killed a lion that had attacked me. Very few men can do that."

"Are you serious?" Jen inquired, not sure whether what she had just heard was said in jest or in seriousness. But then Osak had introduced himself as an African and he spoke with a heavy African accent. So, perhaps he was serious. Osak, sensing he had the ladies engrossed in him now, something he wasn't sure would happen before he made his move to join them, now embellished the false story he had just told.

"I had been out in the African bush to hunt when I saw the beast crouched and ready to pounce. I threw a spear at it, but missed. It then ran over to my position so fast, I barely had a chance to react. It knocked me down, but I had another spear which I stuck deep into its mouth before it could bite me. I got up and ran. I returned the following day and saw the dead lion a few yards from the location of the attack."

As Osak spun his yarn, the two women's mouths were agape in awe. He made such an impression on the women that by the time the club closed in the wee hours of the morning, he had asked for Ingrid's phone number, and she obliged him with the request. That was about 5 years ago now as he reminisced in his home office, deep in thought about the command his mother had given him a short while ago. It dawned on him that he had been away from Ingrid and Felicia, upstairs in the bedroom, for almost an hour.

Osak went back upstairs to check on them. Ingrid was soundly asleep, but Felicia was awake. The pupils of her large eyes rolled from east to west, as she cooed. Osak picked her up and took her into the tastefully furnished living room of plush couches, long flowery window curtains, and a plush carpet.

Osak sat down on a long couch. He cradled Felicia and played with her little hands. As he did this, the matter of her circumcision raised by his mother, came coursing through his brain again, giving him distressing moments. He was not in support of it, but even if he were, there was no chance in hell Ingrid would agree with it. She might even file for immediate divorce for his bringing up such a horrible idea to her. But he was also aware of supernatural forces tied to an ancient tradition in his hometown where he was the heir to the throne. Those supernatural forces could kill him if he refused to do what custom and culture required of him to do. He was thus in a major quandary about what to do. Felicia looked so beautiful and innocent. The thought of any surgical instrument coming close to her body for an anachronistic and cruel procedure like circumcision was unthinkable. Exhausted by the unceasing thoughts, ongoing for a couple of hours now, he fell into a stress induced sleep, still cradling Felicia.

***

Ingrid's yell of his name woke him up. He had been asleep for about a half an hour. Ingrid had herself woken up to discover Felicia missing from beside her on the bed. She had panicked and called Osak's name out loud.

"Do you have the baby with you?" she asked from where she lay in the bedroom.

"I do," Osak replied after being startled seconds earlier by her loud callout of his name. "Are you okay?" he asked.

"Other than an ache here and there, I feel fine," she replied.

Osak got up slowly with Felicia firmly in his arms and made his way to the bedroom upstairs. Ingrid leaned up her back on several pillows. She looked slightly tousled from her ordeal of the past week in labor and childbirth, though her skinned glowed.

"I got to call mom and dad to tell them we are home now," said Ingrid.

Osak placed Felicia inside her crib next to the bed Ingrid laid on. It had been gifted by Jen during a baby shower Jen had organized for her friend a week before Felicia's birth. Jen had encouraged Ingrid along in her relationship with Osak in the early going when Ingrid had doubts about it, particularly whether an interracial love affair would work out for her. It was a big deal because, like Osak, she was dating across racial lines for the first time. When Ingrid decided to introduce Osak to her parents, after a year of their relationship, her trepidation about doing so was assuaged by Jen's support. Ingrid's father, Ronald, had racist tendencies, while her mother, Eunice, did not.

Ingrid picked up her cell phone and placed a call to her mother. The phone rang a few times without being picked up from the other end. Ingrid called again with the same outcome.

"She is probably busy doing something. I'll try again later."

"Sweetheart, can you make me some light soup," she said to Osak. "I am slightly hungry."

"Sure!"

Osak left the bedroom and headed for the kitchen to make Ingrid her soup. Ingrid stretched her neck to catch a glimpse of Felicia, who had fallen asleep. She reached out into a tall shelf next to her bed to retrieve a breast pump. She pulled up her bra and placed the pump next to her right breast to extract breast milk. She had breast fed Felicia directly from her breast during her one week stay at the hospital. She was into the breast pumping activity when her phone rang. It was her mother calling back.

"Hello honey, I missed your call," said Eunice.

"Hi mom!"

Ingrid was the figurative carbon copy of her mother, who was blond haired, tall, of average build, and possessing of a soft featured face. Eunice had a premonition about what the missed call from her daughter was about. She had visited with her at the hospital the day after Felicia's birth when Ingrid was well enough to receive visitors. She had learned Ingrid and her baby would be kept for several days at the hospital. Perhaps they were back from the hospital and Ingrid wanted to let her know about it.

"Are you home now from the hospital?" she asked.

"Yes, mom, we got back from the hospital just this afternoon."

"How are both you and Felicia doing?"

"We are doing okay, mom."

"Is she crying a lot?"

"She is sleeping right now, but she hasn't cried that much."

"I will close the restaurant early tomorrow and come to visit with you," said Eunice.

"How is dad?"

"He is fine. He is at the bank to make some cash deposits. I will come with him for the visit."

"Alright mom, I'll see both of you tomorrow."

"Thank you, honey. Bye!"

Ingrid went back to the breast pumping activity. She constantly eyed Felicia in her crib, making sure she was okay. The brief conversation with her mother was akin to a soothing balm for her body ache. Her mother was her best friend and confidante. She was always there for her in both good and bad times. When confronted with difficult issues, her mother, like a guardian angel, always had a way to help resolve them for her. Eunice was the most optimistic person she had ever known, who had a cheer, a perpetual smile, and ready words of encouragement to beat back gloom and pessimism.

One of the most difficult issues Ingrid had to deal with in her 20 years of life on earth at the time was her interracial relationship. She had thought her platonic relationship with her African friend would wane and they would both drift apart to focus on their respective interests in other areas of their lives. But Osak had persisted and acted towards her in several ways that demonstrated that he wanted more than a platonic relationship. It was very difficult for Ingrid to process all that was happening in the context of the realities Osak was relentlessly creating—the gifts, the words of affection on the phone and in text messages, his assistance with her homework and projects from class, and how powerfully and emotionally he had made love to her the first time, after she had kept the most cherished part of her anatomy from him for months, following the start of their romance. He was patient and never pushed the issue about that. That enamored him to her.

***

Ingrid hailed from a small town in the Northwest, in the state of Washington. Her only exposure to black people, growing up in this town, were the images she saw on television of national political figures, celebrities, athletes and performers. She came physically close to black people later in high school where 5% of the student population were black, and they were from the small community of black residents in the county. Ingrid's mother was open-minded, being descended from a Scandinavian family which was among the early settlers of the State of Washington. Her father, Conrad, had served in the Second World War and had been a command officer in a battalion of black soldiers. He developed camaraderie with his men at a time when such was not common in the US Army. He returned from the war with a changed attitude about race relations in a country rife with racial prejudice. Conrad raised Eunice and three other children to believe in racial tolerance. For several summers, he hosted a number of the black men he commanded in war at his ranch. When Ingrid had approached Eunice about her dilemma with her African friend, she was the perfectly suitable person to help her deal with the situation.

CHAPTER 2

The morning weather was chilly, as light snow had fallen during the night. Eunice and Ronald were about to drive out north to Maryland to visit with their daughter, just back from the hospital with her new baby, their first grandchild. Eunice called Ingrid to tell her they were on their way. Moments later, Ronald started up the car and pulled out of the driveway. Eunice sat in the front passenger seat. The rear seat was jammed with baby food, pampers, baby clothes, and balloons.

Ronald drove slowly through the estate of single family homes where they had lived for 27 years and raised Ingrid and her brother Hans. He soon joined the interstate highway from where the distance to Ingrid and Osak's home would be a 25 minute drive. Eunice's perpetual smile was etched on her face. Ronald's countenance was the opposite. He was a wiry man, seemingly always in a hurry, and serious. He was southern born and had moved to the northwest with his mother and step father as a young man. His mother's abusive relationship with Ronald's alcoholic biological father had ended in a bitter divorce and his mother had been granted custody of Ronald. She met a native Washingtonian serviceman a year later and married him. Several years later, they relocated to the Seattle area where Ronald spent his adolescent years, graduated from high school and college, and started a professional career in the hotel industry as a manager. This entailed him being on the road a lot as he rose in rank and had to supervise various locations of the hotel chain. He typically drove carefully from his days as a supervising hotel manager.

Ronald drove at the speed limit on Interstate 95. Several vehicles wheezed past him at top speed. Eunice did not know what to make of Ronald's serious countenance behind the steering wheel. He had an inscrutable mien, but he was also a loving man. She knew how to crack through that façade of seriousness to engage him in interesting and funny dialogue. But she was also aware that Ingrid's relationship and eventual marriage to Osak was something he had disapproved of and had allowed to bother him for a long time.

During the four years that had elapsed since the marriage, the hurt had slowly healed. He had cut off communications with Ingrid, and only Eunice's reconciliatory persistence ended the feud. But Eunice still suspected that some hurt, diminished as it seemed, was still left inside his soul. Maybe the birth of his first grandchild would flush out the rest of the hurt, she thought, as they motored up the Interstate and the distance to Ingrid's house decreased.

"How do you feel about going to see your granddaughter for the first time?" she asked him, piercing through his serious façade.

"I feel great! I'm looking forward to it."

"That's good!" said Eunice.

The unusual light traffic was a factor in how quick their journey was. Ronald pulled up in front of the house exactly 20 minutes from the time they had left their home in northern Virginia. Osak had spied their arrival from a bedroom window upstairs.

"They're here," he said to Ingrid.

"Oh great! Let them in."

"Of course!"

Osak hurried downstairs to open the door to

let his in-laws in. They exchanged pleasantries as he ushered them in and led them into the living room. Several minutes later, Ingrid emerged from the bedroom with Felicia. She walked down the stairs gingerly, cradling the baby carefully in her arms. Soon she reached the living room and pleasant excitement from her parents erupted. Ingrid passed the baby to Eunice who beamed. Ronald gazed at the baby in amazement. Felicia was neatly wrapped up in blankets and only her pink and cheery face showed. Ronald touched her cheeks and tickled her face. Felicia smiled in response.

Osak served drinks and snacks. He had kept his in-laws pleasant company for about ten minutes when his phone rang. It was Bilky calling. Osak excused himself to take the call. He suspected what the topic of the call was going to be about, and to be certain that the conversation would not be overhead by his wife and in-laws, he went outside to take the call.

"Hello, mama," he greeted.

"Hello son, how are you!"

"I am fine, thank you."

"Son, I called to ask when you are bringing the child for the circumcision so we can prepare ahead of time."

Osak was quiet, for he did not have an immediate response to the question. Bilky continued. "Your father consulted the oracle, as custom required of him to do to find out who among our ancestors had reincarnated in your daughter, and the finding was very surprising. He found out that the matriarch of the community, a woman named Uwa, who with her husband, Iken, settled our community several hundred years ago, and raised eight sons our eight villages are named after today, is the one who reincarnated in your daughter. This is the first time she has come back since her death all those hundreds of years ago. Your daughter is therefore special. She belongs not only to you, but to the entire community. Your father will talk to you about the reincarnation ritual ceremonies and big feast he will lead the community to engage in to welcome back this great matriarchal ancestor to the community."

Osak, still lost for words, listened to his mother, never cutting in to say anything.

"...Although you have named her Felicia, we are naming her Uwa, the name she bore when she first lived on this earth several hundred years ago. The circumcision must be done during the period of the ritual ceremony and feast," She concluded.

"When is this ritual ceremony?" Osak asked.

"No later than one year from the date of her birth," she answered.

"Mama, you are making my life very difficult with this demand."

"How so, son?"

"I won't be able to convince my white wife to go along with a circumcision of Felicia. I told you that the last time"

"Son, is it your wife that will make this decision for you? Are you the man in the marriage or not?"

"Mama, it is more complicated than you think."

"Son, I warned you when you told us you wanted to marry outside your community and marry the white woman. Remember I told you about the high probability of problems with her about your cultural heritage."

"You did, but there are things that are old fashioned which must go, and female circumcision is one of them, mama."

"Is it because the white people said so?"

Bilky shot back. "Why did they bring us Christmas and forced us to believe in Christmas? Is Christmas original to our culture?"

"Mama, religion is different. Besides, Christmas celebrates the birth of Jesus Christ, our Lord and Savior."

Osak's parents were Muslim. Bilky challenged his assertion.

"No, our religion recognizes Him as a Prophet, not the savior of the world. In any case, the whites brought the religion here and you converted to it. Do you know how much pain you caused us by this conversion? The kingmakers were going to strip you from succeeding your father, but he prevailed on them to stand down about it. Now, you are trying to cause another trouble with this circumcision argument."

"Mama, I keep saying to you that this matter is more complicated than you think. It won't be easy for me to comply."

"Son, I insist on my demands being met. Your daughter is not an ordinary human. She is the great matriarchal ancestor, Uwa. The risk of not complying with what tradition and culture demands might make her sick and cause her to return to the realm of the ancestors."

"What does that mean?" Osak asked.

"It means what it means. Figure it out yourself..."

Osak had been outside for about 15 minutes now, on the phone with Bilky. Ingrid spied twice on him from a gap in the window blinds during that period. She observed him animated at times, and she had never seen him that way before. She figured something had to be wrong, perhaps at his office or something else. Whatever it was, she would ask him about it when she got a chance, perhaps after her parents had left.

Osak came back into the house. He had a smile on his face which belied the anguish he felt from the just concluded conversation with Bilky. Ronald and Eunice just continued chatting with him from where they had left off, but Ingrid was a tad reticent to carry on as if all was fine. In her four years of living with her husband, she had come to know what made him tick and what set him off, although occasions like that were extremely rare.

Osak was a devoted husband who adored her. She had been tickled to no end one time when he told her she reminded him of the blond and blue eyed baby dolls his parents bought for his sister as birthday gifts when she was very young. He told her he loved the beauty of those baby dolls probably more than his sister did, never knowing that he would someday marry a grown baby doll in human form. He called her 'my grown baby doll' every now and then to make her laugh. They lived very happily. He maintained a highly successful accounting practice, lived clean, never smoked or drank except red wine in social settings, and exercised regularly in a gym he had set up in the basement of their house.

There was only one thing about Osak she had discovered could pierce his otherwise cool and endearing persona and character, and it pertained to his involvement in a registered association of his kinsfolk in America. He and fellow compatriots from their hometown in Africa resident in America had established the association with a mission of providing developmental assistance to the town and her people. They considered themselves privileged to live and work in the USA. They were thus driven to help their less privileged kinsfolk back home by providing funds to build schools, community health centers, and to implement scholarship programs for the brilliant who couldn't afford to pay their way through college.

To fund these projects and programs, they imposed a mandatory levy on members of the association. The body was run by an elected executive and it met once a month. Osak was a regular at these meetings, for he cared deeply about the less privileged back home. But the meetings tended to be highly contentious, and Osak always came back from them exhausted and at times withdrawn as a consequence of the battles. He would be lively, loving and his funny self before going off to these meetings, but would often return from them in a deep funk that lasted for hours sometimes.

Ingrid, concerned for her husband and what these meetings were doing to his mental health, tried to persuade him to stop attending them. Yes, he could go on sending in his monthly levy, but for the sake of his health, she wanted him to stop going. But Osak kept on attending. And so, one day, just before he was to leave for another monthly meeting, Ingrid hid his car keys and pretended she did not know what had happened to them. Osak looked everywhere in the house but couldn't find them. Ingrid, maintaining her ruse, even helped 'search' for them. Osak was forced to skip the meeting. He was upset that he couldn't attend his cherished association meeting, but he was not as forlorn as he usually was after returning from the meetings. Ingrid figured this was a better alternative deal for him, but she also didn't think she could sustain this extreme measure of stopping him from attending in the future. He could coincidentally lose his keys on the same date and time of his scheduled hometown association meeting one time. But losing them repeatedly would definitely give her up as the 'key snatcher.'

The keys reappeared the next morning after Ingrid 'found' them. He did not suspect anything was amiss, that she had hidden the keys to stop him from attending his hometown association meeting. But Ingrid could not keep secret of what she had done. And so she confessed to him about it. It was done out of concern for his mental health, she had told him. She tried to persuade him anew to stop going to the meetings. They were in the second year of their marriage when this incident had occurred.

Osak's reaction to her admonition and sly confiscation of his car keys was strongly negative. He told her off, warned her never to meddle in anything that involved his African community again, and told her he was prepared to walk away from the marriage over the matter. Although he later apologized for his overreaction, particularly his threat to leave her, the episode was burned in her memory. She learned, hotly dramatic as it had played out, that Osak was cool in everything, just don't mess with his commitment to his quarrelsome kinsfolk's community association.

The animated conversation Ingrid had observed him engage in outside was out of the ordinary, unless it was related to the association, but she doubted such because association business was always conducted at their once monthly meetings. She knew this routine very well. Later that night, after her parents had left to return home, Ingrid asked him about the phone conversation she had seen him so passionately engaged in.

"What was that all about? Are you okay?" she asked.

"Oh that was nothing serious. It was a client whose audit I had done and is due to be picked up tomorrow at the office. We were having a little talk about my fees."

Osak had no option but to lie to Ingrid about

the explosive conversation with his mother. He hadn't even begun to deeply process the demand from his mother to arrive at a firm stand on it. His initial reaction had been to recoil at the demand, but he had also given a brief thought to the alleged supernatural forces involved and the implications. His mother had warned about Uwa (Felicia) returning to the ancestral realm, if she was not circumcised and made to go through a reincarnation rite. He interpreted this warning to mean Felicia's possible death, which would be an unspeakable tragedy, should that occur.

"Did you guys resolve the matter?" Ingrid asked.

"Not quite, but I've asked him to see me in the office tomorrow."

***

Two months elapsed without any calls from Africa for Osak. He thought elatedly that his mother had given up on her command. Then his cell phone rang one night, as he ate dinner with Ingrid. It was his father on the phone. Excusing himself, he stepped outside to talk, suspecting the subject of the conversation would be poisonous to Ingrid's ears. He had the option to talk in his native language, but he had never done that before with Ingrid within earshot. He regarded that as disrespectful to her. Even his kinsfolk in the USA, who called him from time to time when Ingrid was with him, and started up a conversation in their native language, did not receive a reciprocal discourse in the language from him. He spoke back in English.

Outside now, several yards from the porch, and standing on the sidewalk, Osak spoke into the phone.

"Hello father!"

"Hello son, I hope you, your wife and Uwa are fine!"

"Yes, we are! I hope you and mother and everybody else in the family are fine, too!"

"We are, and we are also about to start planning for the ritual ceremony and feast to welcome Uwa back to the community she departed from hundreds of years ago. She may have been born in America, but she is spiritually with us here in the community. I hope you know that?"

"Mama mentioned something along those lines the last time we spoke."

King Ebu had additional information for his

son. "The oracle revealed a lot of things about Uwa's past life we didn't even know. Her birth in America even has a linkage to her past. We were shocked to learn about that."

The discussion of these issues anew two months after the stressful talk with his mother distressed Osak all over again. He had thought the two month hiatus in phone calls from her meant his parents had decided to move on from the matter. But this call definitely demonstrated that was not the case. The claims about Felicia and linkages to some dead ancestor sounded outlandish to his newly cultivated American mindset. He would have believed it before the start of his American experience seven years earlier. Back home in the community that shaped his early life, he had been attuned to the complex esoteric and supernatural laced traditional beliefs of his people. But being away from that community now for seven years, and rooted now in American culture, having received its education and married into it, his connection with the ancient beliefs of his people was now tenuous. But a strand or two of that connection still in his psyche was curious about his father's claim of a linkage of Felicia's birth with the dead ancestor and America. He had to ask his father to elaborate on it.

"What is this linkage you talk about concerning Felicia, the past and America?" he asked.

"Her name is Uwa. You named her Felicia, but she is Uwa and will always be known as Uwa," his father admonished. "...The oracle told us that white people came to our community during the lifetime of Uwa, and that she and Iken, her husband, befriended the leader of those white people who brought them new things from their country. The white people left with one of the couple's eight male children. They promised to educate him in the white man's ways and bring him back. The boy did come back after several years and he had nothing but good things to say about the white man's land. Uwa then vowed to live her next life in the white man's country."

The riveting story made Osak reminisce about his secondary school history class in his country. One such account was about Portuguese explorers who first landed in West Africa in the 15th century and had initially engaged in non human trade with African tribes. A few powerful kings among these tribes had sent their sons to

Portugal to be educated. If the story about Uwa was true, it probably occurred during this period, Osak reasoned, though he was still skeptical about the claim his father was making.

"We are waiting on you to bring her back for the circumcision and the ceremonies," said King Ebu.

Osak's conversation with his father had lasted ten minutes. He came back into the house and rejoined Ingrid in the dining room. He wore a serious mien, and this was not the case before he stepped outside to take the call. Ingrid suspected it had to do with another of his hometown association issues which often sapped him. She asked him about it, even though she knew he didn't like her meddling in such issues.

"I hope it's not your association's issues again that caused this tightness on your face?"

"No it's not."

"What is it then? You were perfectly okay until that phone call."

"I am okay. It's that same client from 2 months ago. He has been a pain. He has complained about sections of my audit, and he still owes me a balance of my fees."

Arising from their dinner about an hour later,

Ingrid, cradling Felicia in her arms, took her into the bathroom to change her diapers. Osak absent mindedly picked up the dishes, walked over to the kitchen, and put them in the dishwasher. He next went into his office to prepare for the next morning at the office, where he had a full schedule, for it was tax filing season again. This was a period that kept him extremely busy and working late nights. Ingrid had another week of maternity leave before returning to work at a law office where she worked as a legal secretary. Osak worked for a couple of hours then came to bed. Ingrid was still awake, as she rocked Felicia to try to make her fall asleep.

When they kissed and said good night to each other, lying on their king sized bed, Osak nursed a slight headache from his earlier conversation with his father. Ingrid slept soundly through the night, but Osak turned and tossed for most of the night.

CHAPTER 3

Osak showed up for work the next morning still nursing a headache. He had taken Tylenol for the headache before driving out to his office. Osak had an office secretary named Barbara. She was white, 22 years old, and fresh out of college with a degree in Business. Barbara did administrative tasks and organized Osak's schedule. Her office was next to Osak's. She could eavesdrop on him if she wanted to. Osak tried to work, but he was distracted for several hours by the pressure mounted on him by his parents over the circumcision issue. Osak needed someone to talk to, preferably from his hometown association.

Just before he called it a day and left for home, he placed a call to a kinsman who was also a member of the hometown association. Ovu, the man Osak called, had come to the USA about 10 years before Osak's arrival. They shared a lot in common, though Ovu was older. They were both accountants, they were married to white women, and they shared the same birthday, a day they often commemorated with an invitation only dinner hosted by their wives, Ingrid and Sarah. Ovu was mild tempered. Osak noticed this quality in him during hometown association meetings, when most members engaged in shouting matches, and Ovu would watch in studied silence. Ovu often upbraided the combatants after tempers had cooled and he was given the floor to speak. He was respected because he was among the older members of the association. Osak had sought occasional advice from him, but they were mostly about professional matters in their common accounting profession. He had never sought personal advice from him before, but he felt the urge to do so now on the circumcision pressure from his parents.

"Hello Ovu," Osak had greeted.

"How are you? This is Osak."

"I am well, thank you. And you?"

"It's well, except for heavy pressure I feel about something, and it's causing me so much distress, I'm not sure about what to do."

"What is it?"

Osak opened up to Ovu for the next 10 minutes about the discussions with his parents and his dilemma.

"What would you advice me to do?" he asked Ovu.

"Well, thanks for deeming me possessing of the wisdom to advice you on such a thorny matter. It's obviously been eating at you from the anguish in your voice."

Ovu had four boys with Sarah, and so had never dealt with this kind of problem before. His boys had all been circumcised, but male circumcision was an optionally acceptable medical procedure.

Ovu continued with his response. "I would have asked you to ignore your parents, were it not for your unique status as a prince and heir to the throne. You are in the special class of people, along with your parents, who are custodians of our culture and heritage. This means that you can't shirk from carrying out what custom demands of you to do, including this circumcision. As abhorrent as it is to me, you have to do it to save yourself from the backlash of supernatural powers associated with our hometown and its culture."

"Ovu, your take on this is a big jolt," said Osak.

"You asked for my reasoned opinion. I gave it to you. I by no means think it will be easy to do, particularly as your wife is white just like mine. I know your wife will probably oppose it very strongly, and her reaction might even get you in trouble for even contemplating such a thing. "

"I think you're very correct about that," said Osak.

"It's a tough situation for you, no doubt about that," said Ovu.

"Give me more options," Osak asked in panic and frustration.

"Well, you could ignore your parents, but with the caveat I gave earlier about a supernatural backlash. You could also lie to them by telling them that you've taken care of it right here in America, and there was no need to return home for it. But this is also problematic because your daughter is supposed to be Uwa reincarnate, and must be taken home for the ritual ceremonies to welcome her back."

Osak sighed aloud such that Ovu could hear him from his end of the line. He sensed Osak's supreme frustration and angst.

"I must confess I don't envy your situation at all, Osak. It's a difficult one, for sure."

"Would you do what you are recommending to me if you were in my shoes?" Osak asked.

"I am not a royal like you, and so will never be confronted with a situation like that. But if I were in your shoes, I would," said Ovu.

The phone conversation was within earshot of Barbara, who heard it all from her adjacent office. Osak, exhausted from the day's work and mentally fatigued from his issues, had kicked his legs up on his desk, switched his cell phone on to speaker mode, and had placed the phone on the desk. Barbara knew Osak's wife had given birth to a baby girl a little more than 2 months ago. She had met Ingrid a number of times when Ingrid had stopped by the office in the downtown area of Washington DC to pick up her husband at the close of the work day. Ingrid worked in the Georgetown area of the city, about a 10 minute distance from Osak's office. Barbara had also seen Ingrid when she was pregnant and had even attended her baby shower. Barbara thought the discussion was bonkers as she listened to it. She had not paid much attention when the conversation had started with mundane stuff about their hometown association's matters. Then the conversation had shifted to circumcision and Ingrid's daughter was mentioned. At that point her jaw dropped, and her ears pecked up figuratively to listen intently.

"Holy shit!" she exclaimed softly when the conversation had ended. Barbara was aware of female genital mutilation and its practice in certain parts of the world, particularly in the developing world in Africa and in the Middle East. She had been shocked to learn from a Turkish friend about the practice in certain traditionalist regions of Turkey, which was a highly developed European country. But carrying out something like that in America would definitely be illegal which could cause the government to seize the child from her parents. And so she hoped Ingrid would block it if the issue ever came up.

***

Felicia was baptized in the sixth month of her birth. The event took place at the local Catholic Church, followed by a party at Osak and Ingrid's home attended mainly by the kinsmen of Osak and their spouses. This was the second time Osak's kinsmen would be hosted at an event in his home, the first being their house warming party which had taken place two years earlier. Ingrid recalled that even though they had been invited to make merry and celebrate with her and Osak on the purchase of their new house, but they had also brought with them their association's issues, and a few people had quarreled. That was her first time of noticing the strident passion in them about issues concerning their association and the source of her husband's mental exhaustion after his return from their meetings.

Felicia was rolled into the basement in her stroller to be seen and appreciated by the party guests before things got busy with music, drinking and partying. Sarah, Ovu's wife, was there with Ovu and she quickly bonded with Ingrid and two other white women from Ingrid's office. The Africans spoke in their language, effectively shutting off conversation with the Americans. So the four white women congregated at the far end of the basement and made lively banter.

Sarah and Ovu had been on a safari to Kenya the previous year and she regaled the women about her experience, particularly a fight she had observed between a python and an adolescent male leopard. The leopard instigated the fight by thinking the big snake would make a nice dinner. It attempted to bite the snake which reacted so fast and coiled its powerful length around the leopard within seconds. The leopard struggled mightily to escape the grip, and was fortunate to do so. But it kept harassing the snake until it slithered into a hole in the ground.

"Wow!" that must have been quite a sight, said Joana, Ingrid's office mate. "I'd love to go on one of these safaris."

"But here is a strange story my husband told me about pythons: in his African hometown, it is revered as a sacred animal that they do not kill. Pythons come freely into homes and depart as they please. They harm no one. Anyone who killed a python was subjected to banishment from the community until they paid diviners heavy sums to cleanse the land of the sacrilege they had committed. My husband does not think anyone in the community has any memory of the last time a python was killed."

The women's mouths were agape as Sarah told the story.

"I thought pythons ate anything that's living,

including people," said Joana.

"Apparently not in this African community," said Sarah.

"Have you been there before?" asked Frida, Ingrid's other office mate.

"Not yet, we plan to do so next year."

Joana had been nodding to the DJ's selections. The women appeared to be itching to dance. Ingrid led the way to the dance floor where they gyrated for several minutes to a mix of rock and African music. They had company in several others who had been on the floor for over a half hour jamming excitedly to the music. At the other end of the basement, a group of Osak's kinsmen conversed over the din of the music. They were four in number. A burly bearded man was speaking.

"What is he going to do about the girl's circumcision?" he asked his colleagues.

"What do you mean what is he going to do?" a baldheaded slim man retorted. "Did you do that to your own daughters, who were all born here in America?" he asked rhetorically. "Why raise such a useless issue here?"

"Well, I am not a prince like he is, so I am not under any obligation to have it done to my daughters," protested the bearded man.

The third man in the conversation was heavily mustachioed. He stroked it nervously, as he opined in support of the bearded man.

"I had two girls before coming to America, and the procedure was done to both of them. It is our custom and culture, which no one should condemn or take away from us."

The bald headed man countered. "I know you have three girls. Your last girl was born right here in America just last year. Did you do that to her, too?" he asked with a look of scorn on his face.

"No!"

"Why not?"

"Well, we couldn't do it because it is supposed to be illegal here, and I thought it was too expensive to fly her, her mother and me home just so we could do it. I hope she doesn't become promiscuous because she isn't circumcised."

"The last sentence in your statement is total bullshit!" protested the bald headed man. "Why do you pin promiscuity on only women? What about men? Study after study has not established more propensities for promiscuity in women than in men. If women should lose their clitoris based on your unfounded claim, then men should lose their tools too, because women are no more promiscuous than men are."

There was laughter amidst the charged conversation.

The fourth man in the group was Osak's close friend, Ovu, who weighed in with a comment.

"I think it's a very difficult issue for Osak to deal with. He will make the decision he thinks is best for him."

"You have no opinion on what he should do?" the beaded one asked.

"Again he will make the best decision for himself and his family," Ovu insisted.

"You're always on the fence," the bearded one shot back.

The mustachioed man was the newest member in the group, having arrived in America only two years before. He did not therefore know Ovu that well when he asked what everyone thought was a silly question. Ovu looked older, and the mustachioed man had imagined Ovu had both male and female children.

"I bet your kids are all circumcised," he stated, rhetorically.

"Of course they all are," said Ovu.

"Then why are you on the fence about what Osak should do? You are older than all of us here in this group. Older people have a greater responsibility to promote our culture regardless of where we live in the world outside our ancestral homeland."

The bearded one jumped in. "Mr. Ovu has four 4 boys. He has no girl and therefore has never been confronted with this issue before. He has the luxury to sit on the fence"

"Oh, okay! That explains it," said the mustachioed man after learning about Ovu's family. "My earlier assumption had been wrong."

The party now roared, as Osak and Ingrid grooved to a popular African tune. Ingrid used to be lost in the kinds of moves that rhymed with the rhythm of African music, but she learned the right moves over time, as she attended parties hosted by her husband's kinsfolk to celebrate a graduation, a birthday, a wedding, or a baptism like the one she and Osak hosted now. She thoroughly enjoyed herself at these parties. She was in awe of the members of the association, who were high achievers. They were physicians, lawyers, nurses and many other progressive things. They all seemed to know why they were in a land of opportunity as America, and they took full advantage of it to get educated and raise solidly middle class families. They were very good people, who were upwardly mobile. Her only issue with them was the highly contentious meetings they often had relative to their developmental aspirations for their ancestral hometown in Africa.

Osak had once taken her along to one of these meetings in the first year of their marriage. The spouse of a member was an automatic member by virtue of the association constitution, and had voting rights. Ingrid observed first hand, the dynamics of the back and forth that characterized these meetings. After the President, an elderly grey haired man, had gaveled the gathering to order and an opening prayer was said, pinkish brown nuts the size of chestnuts Osak had told her were called kolanuts were served. She had tried eating one before, as Osak loved to munch on them occasionally, but it had been too bitter and she had spit it out. A young man passed the kolanuts around. He got to her and Osak, who picked a nut from a wide and shiny tray. She demurred, but before the young man moved on, Osak asked to be allowed to take

Ingrid's share. He now had two nuts and within seconds, was crunching them in his mouth, making a loud crunchy sound.

The President called up the first substantive issue on the agenda after the last person had been served a kola nut, and it was about whether to renovate a 70 year old secondary school in their hometown, built during colonial times by Christian missionaries, or demolishing it and building a new one. A dichotomy of views soon emerged on the issue, and they engaged in at times very loud argument. Two men had almost come to blows on the matter and had to be restrained. Hours were spent on the issue to the neglect of the rest of the agenda, but in the end, a vote taken on the issue was won by those in favor of tearing down the old structure and building a new school.

On their way home, after the meeting had gone over its scheduled period by several hours, Ingrid told him she thought the fuss was all unnecessary, considering that a vote had been planned all along. Why hadn't the debate proceeded decorously without the rancor she had witnessed?

"We practice our democracy like that. It is

no different from American democratic practice, you know," said Osak.

"I would disagree with you on that," Ingrid retorted.

Osak was an ardent student of American history. He had read up a lot about America after his decision to move there for higher education. He was particularly enamored of Abraham Lincoln, America's 16th President who freed the slaves. He recalled reading Lincoln's biography and learning about how the slavery issue had caused so much national heartburn such that a Senator, who had supported abolishing the cruel commerce in human beings, was attacked for holding that position by a Congressman on the other side of the issue and nearly killed, and the assault had occurred inside the US Capitol.

"What about that?" Osak asked Ingrid, who smiled.

"That happened so long ago," she countered. "America is a much different place today."

The basement started to empty out in the wee hours of the morning. Felicia's baptism party had been a smash thoroughly enjoyed by the attendees. Before activities were formally closed, Osak had asked Ovu to give the vote of thanks.

Ingrid and Osak thereafter made small talk with their guests as they departed one after another. Ingrid soon went upstairs, leaving Osak with the last one or two people left to depart. Ovu was one of them and he had a question for Osak before leaving.

Ovu pulled Osak aside to ask if he had made a decision about the circumcision matter. Was he going along with the option of claiming falsely to his parents about doing the procedure in America, or would he take Felicia home for it, he queried.

"Ovu, how can I even do this? I cannot tell Ingrid about it without her probably 'murdering' me. I can't lie to my parents about the procedure being done here because this thing about reincarnation rite requires of Felicia being taken there for that activity. My only option looks like me taking Felicia there and pretending to be doing so to introduce her to her grandparents, but I'm not sure Ingrid will let me do that, as Felicia is still a baby."

Ovu's face bore a sign of anguish for his friend who equally displayed a pained visage about his dilemma.

"She might agree if we all go together, so she'd be sure that Felicia would be properly cared for, but I am pretty sure she will resist any attempt to take Felicia from her for circumcision. I am also leaning towards ignoring my parents henceforth. I might even cease communicating with them."

"You can't do that Osak! What about your princely status as heir to the throne. Are you going to throw that away by cutting off from your parents and your roots?"

"I would, for the sake of my wife and daughter," said Osak, seeming now to take a firm stand on the matter for the first time.

The conversation between the two men lasted for over a half an hour, as Sarah waited in the car for Ovu. They were the last of the party guests to leave because of the impromptu conversation. Sarah was sleepy and longed to get in her bed. She was thus slightly irritated at her husband for keeping her waiting in the car while he talked the night away with his friend. She tooted the car horn a couple of times in frustration. Ovu's attention was drawn the second time, compelling him to bring the conversation to an end.

"Okay, my friend," he said, as they both took slow steps towards his car. "Let's talk tomorrow.

Goodnight!"

"Thanks for coming. I appreciate the company," said Osak.

Ovu got in the car, started it up, and slowly drove off, as Osak waved goodbye.

"You took so long," complained Sarah. "I need to go to bed."

"I'm sorry about that," Ovu apologized.

"What were you guys talking about?"

"Nothing much, we were rubbing minds about the state of our hometown association and our quadrennial elections coming up soon."

Ovu had lied to Sarah, for he couldn't guarantee that the circumcision issue wouldn't be leaked to Ingrid, if he had been truthful and told Sarah about it. Ovu felt slightly sleepy from the wine he had consumed at the party, yet forty minutes of driving lay between him and their home on the outskirts of Baltimore City.

The roads were almost deserted at close to 3am in the morning, as Ovu drove about 12 miles above the speed limit. He had been driving for about 30 minutes with another 10 to go when he approached a speed trap set up by a patrol officer holding a radar gun in his right hand. Ovu braked abruptly to slow down, propelling the seat-belted

Sarah forcefully forwards, which woke her up, startled.

"What's going on?" she asked, as Ovu slowly drove past the patrol officer, who made menacing eye contact, but fortunately passed on coming after Ovu to conduct a traffic stop.

"That was close," he said to Sarah.

"Were you speeding?"

"I guess I was! I've never received a speeding ticket before, and this is my 17th year in America. I like that unblemished record and want to keep it that way."

Ovu pulled in front of their garage several minutes later. Their children, ages 4, 8, 10 and 12 were sleeping soundly when the automatic garage door had opened. Johnny, the 12 year old was awakened by the noise and he opened his upstairs bedroom window to look. He had been traumatized a year ago when their home had been burglarized by amateur burglars, who had pried open a backdoor to the fenced backyard. It had happened in the morning. The burglars had assumed the occupants of the home were either at work or at school, if the owners had school age children. They had thus struck at that time of the morning, but their assumption was off because

Johnny had the flu and had stayed home from school. He was laid up in his bed upstairs when he heard the strange noise akin to a key being unlocked with great difficulty. He got up and slowly made his way downstairs to investigate. There, he came face to face with the burglars, who had just gained entry. They were two grown boys who turned around quickly and escaped through the same backdoor they had broken and entered from. Johnny quickly called his dad and the police, who arrived on the scene within minutes. Ovu was mightily glad that his son was unharmed, but he also admonished him for failing to turn on the home alarm system while he slept.

CHAPTER 4

Osak cut off communications with his parents over the circumcision issue. He refused to take their calls and never made any calls to them. He made up his mind to give up his right of succession to the traditional stool of his hometown his family had held on to since the community was founded by Uwa and Iken. He was proud of his direct lineage to both historical figures, but he loved his wife and daughter and was not going to succumb to a cultural practice that could destroy his marriage to the woman he loved. Ambivalence got the best of him at times such that he would fleetingly think about going forward with the circumcision, as grotesque as it would be, if he could keep his princely status and succeed his father to the throne. The wound would heal after all. But his main worry was his beloved wife and the hurt the issue would create in their relationship, for he was dead sure the matter would create an irreparable rift in their marriage. Maybe Ingrid could be warmed up to the idea by watching a documentary with her to gauge her reaction, he thought.

It was a crazy idea, but there was no harm in trying it out. At this point Felicia was nine months old, just three months shy of the one year deadline his mother had given him to have her circumcised. There were no rental outlets that had a documentary film on female genital mutilation, and so Osak turned to YouTube where he searched and found a documentary and an African themed film on it. He copied both films and burned them on CD-ROMS. The days went by as they still adjusted to the routine of dealing with a new baby.

Ingrid was fully back at work now after her maternity leave. Care for Felicia was a challenge as it was, nationwide, for young professional couples like them. They could afford a nanny, but they were also afraid of nanny abuses, which were frequently reported in the news lately. Ingrid worked out a deal with her parents whereby she and Osak dropped off Felicia with Eunice, who babysat her until she was picked up again in the late evening. Eunice's duties at the restaurant she owned with her husband were taken up by an extra hire whose salary was paid by Ingrid and Osak. Eunice changed her hours at the restaurant to reflect the deal and only worked there on weekends when Felicia was cared for by her parents.

The arrangement was punishing in the context of the mileage they covered each day. At 6am, every morning from Monday to Friday, they drove for 30 minutes, at times up to an hour, depending on the crush of rush hour traffic, to Arlington Virginia to drop off Felicia then drove through the notorious northern Virginia traffic into Washington DC to their respective offices for work. At about 5pm, they headed south into Virginia to pick up Felicia before spending another hour on the intestate expressway to get home. It was exhausting, but they would have it no other way to get the top class babysitting care their daughter deserved.

Felicia turned 10 months on a week Ingrid's employers informed her about a legal secretaries' conference they wanted to send her to in

Colorado. She would be away for a week. Osak and Felicia would be alone during the period. Ingrid thought about asking her mother to move in during her one week absence from home, but decided against the idea. On the eve of her departure for the conference, as she spent a quiet Sunday afternoon with Osak, he asked her to watch a documentary with him.

Osak had set up a private TV room in the basement when they had moved in and had installed a large plasma TV on the wall. There were plush sofas and lacquered coffee tables in the red carpeted room. The walls were painted purple, Ingrid's favorite color. Osak opened up a bottle of champagne and served Ingrid fresh popcorn. He slotted a CD-ROM, on which had been burned the documentary, into a DVD player, pushed the play button and sat next to Ingrid to watch the film. A nondescript shack in a slum out of a developing country was the first image to come into view. A young woman was shown in tears, while a baby's loud cries were heard behind a curtain where a circumcision was presumably going on. The sobbing woman was the mother of the crying child. Minutes later, she was seen being interviewed.

"Why were you sobbing?" they asked her.

"Because my daughter was going through a very painful thing that will cause her to lose a lot of blood, and I was feeling for her."

"But why did you agree to it?" she was asked.

"Because it is something in our culture we have always done to girls, so I had no choice but to agree to it."

"Do you support this practice?" she was asked.

"No, I do not like it at all, but I can't by myself challenge the practice. I am only a woman. I don't have any voice in things like this about our culture. It is the men who decide."

"How many women do you know that have the same feelings as you do about this practice?"

"Some women support it, but most women I know here in our village are against it. Some girls have died from this practice..."

Osak spied Ingrid's countenance from the corner of his eyes as the film rolled on, and her taut and chagrined face was clear even in the slightly darkened room. Ingrid was clearly in distress as the images were shown on the TV screen.

"This is awful," Ingrid let out after having

seen too much, including several more minutes of howling babies, interviews of adult women who had been circumcised as kids, and interviews with the men who did the circumcision and the nonsensical reasons they gave for the practice. They were all old men, and this enraged her further. She then became curious about Osak's interest in the documentary.

"What is the purpose of this film?" she asked him. "Why did you screen it?"

"I just wanted us to watch it, to be informed about the cruel practice, and to appreciate the great American civilization we are living in right now, which will never tolerate such a practice."

"I have heard about female genital mutilation before," said Ingrid. "...I always thought it was awful, but this is my first time seeing a documentary on it."

From Ingrid's reaction to the documentary, Osak didn't think she could bear watching the featured film on the subject, burned into the second CD-ROM he had wanted to screen, and so he cancelled showing it. His general assessment of the situation after watching the film with Ingrid was never to suggest to her that Felicia be put through the procedure. The case was therefore closed on the issue. His parents could apply pressure on him as much as they wanted, but he would continue to ignore them. They ate an early dinner after which Ingrid went to bed early. She was scheduled to leave for her conference by a morning flight and she wanted a full night's rest.

Ingrid was up early the next day to prepare for her trip to Colorado. By 7am, she was seated in the front passenger seat of Osak's car, and Felicia was in her car seat, strapped to a rear passenger seat. Osak pulled out of the garage shortly after 7.15 am for the one hour drive to the Baltimore/Washington International Airport for Ingrid's 10am flight.

"I'll miss the two of you."

"We'll miss you too, "said Osak.

Osak kept up with the speed of traffic on the Baltimore/Washington Parkway towards the airport. Ingrid was relaxed during the ride, except for a short period of time when her mind had wandered to the documentary they had seen the previous night. The harrowing experiences of the screaming babies behind the dirty curtains and their sobbing mothers had bothered her sleep, and she hadn't slept well. Why such cruelty over stupid beliefs, she wondered. One particular statement from one of the old men infuriated her. Asked by the filmmaker what the purpose was for the practice, the old man had answered that the practice was necessary to curb the sexual urges of females. As the clitoris was the source of those urges and sexual pleasure, there was need to cut it off. There would be too many promiscuous women walking around with excited clitorises, if circumcisions were not performed, the old man had stated further with a flourish.

What arrant bullshit! Ingrid had thought of the statement. To another question posed to the old man Ingrid had now started to hate with a passion, even though she probably would never ever meet him in person, he had answered it in the same atrociously condescending manner towards women. The question was why men were entitled to sexual pleasure if they deprived women of the same by removing a part of the flesh which gave them sexual pleasure. Shouldn't sexual pleasure be a mutual thing, the old man was asked, and he answered that women were created to give birth, not to derive sexual pleasure from sex. Only males had a right to pleasure.

"I want to grab his thin neck and wring it around until it's broken," Ingrid whispered to herself, furious.

"Do you remember what that scraggly and unkempt old man said in that documentary yesterday?" She asked Osak.

"What part of his statement do you ask of?"

"Where he carried on about why only men were entitled to sexual pleasure, and women becoming loose if uncircumcised," Ingrid clarified.

"Yes, I now remember. What about the statement?"

"Do you agree with that?"

"Of course I do not."

"That film appeared to have been shot in Africa. Is that the belief over there among most of the men, and is this a widespread practice over there?" she asked.

"No and No," he replied.

"That circumciser is evil and should roast in hell for all the physical and psychological damage he has caused the girls he put under his barbaric knife," said Ingrid in condemnation. "He probably has been doing this all his life. Can you imagine the thousands he has scarred for life?"

Osak had no reaction to her statement, but it was strongly clear from Ingrid's railing against the circumciser that the issue was a no go area. He maintained the speed of traffic as he neared the departure terminal where several vehicles were lined up, dropping off travelers. He came to a stop and they both stepped out of the car. Osak retrieved Ingrid's suitcase from the trunk and handed it to her. She spent a couple of minutes caressing Felicia who had fallen asleep in her car seat. She tarried for a few minutes to make light talk with Osak. There was still an hour of time left before her flight's departure.

Finally, she had to go. "Be well! Take good care of Felicia. I will see you in a week's time."

"...Safe journey, and please call when you arrive," he told her.

They kissed one last time and she turned around and walked into the terminal.

***

Ingrid's travel for her work was the first time they would be apart since they were married a little over 3 years ago. Osak didn't anticipate being lonesome, as he had his daughter with him who would need his full attention. He decided he would work from home for half of the time Ingrid would be gone, and that way spend more time with Felicia. It was a good balance until Ingrid's return. Barbara would run the office, doing routine tasks and managing his client schedule. He returned home from the airport and within an hour found himself sorely missing Ingrid already.

Ingrid arrived at her Colorado destination by the early afternoon and checked into a hotel. She next called Osak to inform him of her arrival. He placed Felicia's face next to his phone, so her baby sounds could be heard by Ingrid, who was excited and tried to talk to her.

"Hi sweetheart," she spoke into the phone to Felicia's baby sounds. "Sweetheart, I hope she is fine. Have you given her food?" she asked Osak.

"She is great. She just ate and she ate a lot."

"...Well, I just got to the hotel literally minutes ago. There is a meet and greet later this evening. I think I will skip that and get some rest before the first day of the conference tomorrow."

"It's a good idea. Better be refreshed before the main thing tomorrow," said Osak in encouragement.

They chatted on the phone for another half hour until Ingrid asked to break off so she could take her rest. He also had some work to do in his home office.

Osak worked for several hours in his home office preparing audits and other financial documents for his clients. He was tired by about 9pm and decided to close up. He bathed Felicia, changed her diapers, fed her again and put her to bed. He then made himself a meatloaf dinner, drank a can of coke and retired for the night.

Osak was asleep for several hours when he suddenly woke up in a rough and sweaty nightmare. He was about to be stabbed in the dream, but he had willed himself to open his eyes simultaneous with him shouting at the top of his voice. Drenched in night sweat, he sat up and tried to make sense of the dream in which an old woman, unimaginably tall at over nine feet in height, with a glowing red face and eyes that shone like stars, had told him she was Felicia, and that he should get on with the reincarnation rite in his ancestral hometown, or she would return to the realm of their ancestors. She disappeared immediately after speaking those words and was replaced by a large man who lunged at Osak with a knife. That was what had stirred Osak to get up, shouting as he did so.

Osak was frightened to no end by the dream. He rarely had nightmares. The last time he had an awful dream like that was in high school, when his maternal grandmother had died in the dream, although she was still alive in actuality. His father attributed the dream to malaria when he had told him about it. He certainly had no malaria last night to have experienced this latest nightmare and it disturbed his mind greatly. He continually looked over his shoulders and around him to make sure that the strange old woman in the dream was not lurking around somewhere in the bedroom.

The old woman's admonition about a reincarnation rite his parents had previously told him about flummoxed him a great deal. The correlation was amazing and appeared supernatural. His parents had warned him about Uwa returning to where she had come from if he did not comply with their directives. This warning seemed to connote the possible death of Felicia. Now, the old woman had repeated the same thing, and this made Osak to fear for Felicia's life. He hurried to where she lay in her crib and touched her face to make sure she was still alive. She was indeed still breathing and soundly asleep. Osak heaved a sigh of relief then returned to his bed, where he sat up again for several hours, unable to fall asleep. He remained in this state until it was mercifully daylight again and the start of a new day.

Osak started the new day still mightily worried about the dream and what it portended. Were the words of the old woman and the man who tried to stab him revelations of terrible things about to occur in his life? He was ambivalent about dreams being a foreteller of events in the future of a person's life, but in light of the conversations he'd had with his parents surrounding Felicia, he was unnerved by this dream. The nightmare he had in high school involving his maternal grandmother came to mind again. Although, his 'dead maternal grandmother' in that dream was incongruous with reality, in the sense that she was still a living person when he had woken up, and even went on to live for another 20 years, he could recall one or two dreams which did correspond to worldly reality, particularly the one in which he had failed a crucial test required for his college admission in America. That test, called 'Test Of English As A Foreign Language' (TOEFL), was required of all prospective foreign students to pass before admission by American colleges. He had studied hard for it, but he failed to pass it in the dream and in reality. He was compelled to retake it.

Osak checked up on Felicia who was wide awake now and uncomfortable because her diapers were wet. He changed her, gave her a quick bath, and made her food. The phone rang and it was Ingrid who was calling to check up on them. They spoke for several minutes before Ingrid had to disengage to attend her first presentation. The phone rang again just as he had just hung up with Ingrid, and it was Eunice on the other end.

"Hi Osak!" she greeted.

"Good morning madam Eunice! How are you!"

"I am well, how is my grandbaby?"

"She is fine and very bubbly this morning."

"That's good. Can you bring her over at least for one day before Ingrid gets back?"

"Sure! When do you want me to do that?"

"Ingrid gets back next Monday. You can bring her over this coming weekend and pick her up on Sunday."

"That will work. I'll see you then."

"Thank you, Osak. Take care!"

"Thank you Madam Eunice!"

Osak went back to tending to Felicia, changing her clothes and propping her up on a high seat in his office. He then turned on his computer to start the day's work—it was a Tuesday and he was working from home. He struggled to concentrate, but that dream wouldn't go away from his mind. Spooking him even further earlier in the morning, when he looked in the mirror as he shaved, was an image of a woman in a halo standing behind him. He turned around to look but found no one there. He thought he was hallucinating, but the eerie scene occurred again. Again, he looked behind him and the image was gone.

Felicia's baby noises were pleasant to his ears. His melancholy was soothed by them. The paradox of the joy he derived from her presence, yet her whole being and existence causing him distress was strange. He thought it was unfair. Reaching for his cell phone, he tapped on Ovu's phone number. Ovu picked up and greeted.

"Hello Osak, how have you been my friend?"

"Terrible!" said Osak in a pained voice.

"What's going on?"

"I had this really awful dream last night, and this morning, another terrifying incident occurred while I was shaving. I've tried to make a meaning of them, but my fright is not letting my brain process properly.

Osak told Ovu the nightmarish details of what had happened to him in the last several hours, and asked Ovu about what he thought he should make of them. Ovu started off by reminding Osak of the advice he had given him on the circumcision issue. He was convinced that the dream and the vision of the woman in the bathroom were revelations from the supernatural world to Osak to comply with the directives his parents had given him about his daughter's circumcision and her reincarnation rite.

"I have no doubt that the old woman you saw in that dream was Uwa, and her message to you in that dream was to present Felicia for the reincarnation rite back home, and to comply with everything else our traditions require to be done about her, including her circumcision," said Ovu. "The vision you saw was probably her again, projecting to you her insistence for you to proceed with what she had told you in the dream without delay."

"Ovu, I cannot do this without irreparably harming my marriage to the woman I truly love. Why am I presented this dreadful choice of either my daughter or my wife in order for me to live my life happily? It's not fair."

"Osak, you are a prince of the kingdom. Your life is not the same as that of commoners in the community like me. But I can recommend a radical way of dealing with this matter without any harm to your marriage."

"Please tell me, what is it?"

"You can manufacture a ruse that separates your wife and you for about a week or so, during which you would have custody of Felicia. You will then fly her out of the country for the circumcision and the reincarnation rite, and fly right back after."

Ovu, what you have detailed here is wild and not feasible. There is no way one week will be enough for all this. Felicia's wound from this circumcision will take longer than a week to heal, and Ingrid will find out."

"The separation ruse can be planned to last for more than two weeks then," said Ovu.

"Ingrid will still find out about the missing clitoris,"

"Her finding out is no big deal," Ovu retorted. "If she asks about it, you can tell her you don't know what happened to it. It could have atrophied as a natural occurrence..."

Osak found Ovu's fantastic plan intriguing,

but he also thought that the component about flying Felicia out of the country would be difficult to do. He could construct a ruse that would allow him to be alone with Felicia. It could even occur during a professional trip out of town by Ingrid, but when that would occur and everything else being perfectly in place was anyone's guess.

Ovu helped him to fine tune the plan in the course of two hours of discussion. Osak promised to get back to him as needed as he tried to put the plan together. The week went by slowly until it was weekend again. Osak looked forward to Ingrid's return in the next couple of days on Monday. It was a Saturday, and he called Eunice to make sure he could still bring Felicia over as had been discussed earlier in the week. Eunice was still fine with it.

Osak took Felicia to her grandmother later in the afternoon. Ronald was at the restaurant. Eunice, who was home alone, was delighted to see her son-in-law and granddaughter. When Ingrid had first brought Osak to her and Ronald, she had been open-minded about their daughter's interracial relationship, unlike her husband, who acted coldly towards Osak. Ingrid became distressed about it as the relationship blossomed, but Eunice's counsel and support soothed her mind. Osak too sensed the tension on that first day and felt ill at ease inside the home. He feared for his life, perhaps irrationally. An aspect of American culture he knew very well growing up back home, particularly when he started reading voraciously about America, was gun violence. He thought Ronald would shoot him. Midway through the visit, he had asked to speak to Ingrid just outside the house. There he told her his concern and his desire to leave immediately. Ingrid was appalled and scolded him for the first time for sounding alarmist. Yes, she had also detected the poisonous chemistry between her dad and Osak, but thoughts of murder in Osak's head was going too far and she assured him there was no 'chance in hell' it would happen.

Here now with his daughter to visit with Eunice, he briefly recalled the tension on that first visit a few years ago which had perturbed him.

"What can I offer you?" Eunice asked. "There is beer, juice and soft drinks," said Eunice, as Osak handed her Felicia.

"Orange Juice should be fine."

Eunice, with Felicia in her arms, walked into the kitchen and opened a double door refrigerator from where she retrieved a gallon of juice and poured out a glass for Osak. She also made him a turkey sandwich.

"...Ingrid returns on Monday, right?"

"Yes, I am expecting her back on Monday evening," said Osak."

"You can leave Felicia here with me for the rest of the weekend and Monday. You guys can pick her up on Tuesday after work."

Osak stayed for about two hours then excused himself to leave.

"I'll see you guys on Tuesday," said Eunice as Osak said his goodbyes.

"...Certainly! Thanks for the sandwich. Goodbye!"

***

Osak arrived home about an hour later. He was all by himself in the house for another day until Ingrid's return. He thought about honing up on the plan Ovu had shared with him earlier, and there was no better time to do it than now with all the time in the world in his hands, with no one around as a distraction. But after thinking deeply about it, he decided to abandon the plan. He would ignore whatever mysterious revelations had been conveyed in the dream and the phantasmagoric image during his shave. He figured diving into his work would help to erode the scary images in his subconscious about the old woman. There was a lot of work he brought home with him for the weekend, anyway.

CHAPTER 5

Felicia fell seriously ill a few days after turning one year old. She had been a very healthy and happy child before coming down with what had initially seemed like a seasonal cold. It had started with a fever, which Ingrid also thought was caused by her teething. Felicia was up to date in her vaccinations. Ingrid treated her with baby fever-reducing medication and made sure that she was properly hydrated. Felicia still ailed after two days of this treatment. Ingrid had to take time off work to take her to the hospital and devote personal time to her. Felicia got better after several days of treatment and follow up care, and Ingrid went back to work.

A month after Felicia's first major illness, she fell sick again, and this required her admission for a rare disorder, a situation which caused extreme stress and anxiety in Osak and Ingrid. Osak suspected that her illness had a linkage with the circumcision matter, the mysterious things his parents had told him about her birth, the nine feet tall old woman in his dreams, and what she had said to him. For the first time, he felt strongly that the dream he had was a premonition of what his daughter was now going through. A remedy might after all be found in her circumcision and performance of her reincarnation rite, but convincing Ingrid about them was probably futile and dead on arrival. She would be appalled at the pagan nature of it all, and never agree to some pagan ceremony in Africa.

Osak had not really bothered to introduce Ingrid to his parents because of their initial reticence in supporting his decision to marry her. In all the calls he made to them, and the calls from them to him, even before Ingrid gave birth, he had allowed Ingrid just one time to talk to his father, the least opposed to his marriage decision. The conversation had been short because Ingrid's American accent was difficult for King Ebu to understand. Osak, in retrospect, now thought a relationship with his parents could've given them a chance to persuade her to go along. It probably was too late now to start building a relationship between them towards attaining that purpose. Even then, there was no certainty it would work, more so as Felicia was now sick. Ingrid's motherly instinct would probably oppose jettisoning Western medicine for unproven African remedies concocted by witch doctors.

Osak and Ingrid took turns visiting Felicia as she lay in the hospital. Eunice visited her often, and practically lived there to help take care of her. Eunice revealed to the couple that the same disorder Felicia was diagnosed of having had once been found in her own mother, Felicia's great grandmother, and that she had recovered from it to live until she was 90 years old. She assured them that Felicia would come out of it in the end. Osak was not inclined to believe his mother in law. This illness, juxtaposed to the mysterious stuff from his parents and his dreams could not just be ascribed to mere coincidence, he thought. Ovu's plan came into mind again. He felt anew that he could pull it off and save his daughter without significant repercussions on his marriage. The plan needed a revisit and a sharpening of its objectives and execution strategy.

Osak called up Ovu a week later on a Saturday morning. Ingrid and Eunice were away at the hospital visiting with Felicia. At this point, she had been hospitalized for about a month. Ovu was out at a restaurant with his family to celebrate his wife's birthday. Osak's call had come in as the birthday food was about to be served.

"Hello! Ovu."

"Hello my friend," Ovu greeted back.

"Do you have a few minutes?" Osak asked.

"Yes, I do. What's happening?"

Ovu wanted to have the discussion away from the earshot of Sarah after suspecting that the discussion was probably going to be about Osak's daughter. He excused himself to go outside the restaurant to take the call.

"Ovu, my daughter is down, and has been so for some time now."

"What ails her?" Ovu asked.

"The diagnosis is a rare genetic disorder. I've never heard of it before," said Osak.

"Osak, all that's going on in your life about this your daughter is unfortunate, But in my opinion, that diagnosis is incorrect. I think she has an ailment of the spirits caused by supernatural forces working with Uwa, who reincarnated in your daughter."

"You know, Ovu, My mind has been stuck on that belief as well since she became seriously ill." Ovu continued. "The dream you had and that vision in the bathroom were all warnings, and they occurred many months ago. Not heeding to these warnings has now brought you all this grief. I urge you to take quick action to save your daughter, Osak..."

Ovu's conversation with Osak was another long conversation, and lately they tended to occur in the middle of one activity or another with Sarah, who had started to get annoyed about it. The birthday meal had been served by the time Ovu came back into the restaurant, and had been on the table for about a half an hour. The kids wanted to dive into the food, but had to be restrained by Sarah until their dad had come back to pray before they ate. Sarah was not enthused about Ovu's long absence and she let him know it.

"We've been waiting for you. The food is getting cold!"

"Sorry about that!" Ovu apologized.

"Osak calls you at odd times, and your conversations are often long. Is anything going on?" Sarah asked.

"There is nothing going on. We are both accountants and we share information about the latest laws, regulations, and current trends in the profession. Our conversations focus on these matters, primarily, Sarah"

Ovu still feared Osak's issues would be leaked to Ingrid should Sarah learn about them. The untoward consequences of such a leak could only be imagined. Hiding the facts from her, as uncomfortable as he felt about it because of the dishonesty involved, was thus necessary.

Sarah had a hunch about something going on, perhaps innocuous at the very least, and insidious at worst. But she had never known her husband of 13 years to be a bad person. They had met in college, where Ovu regularly appeared on the Dean's List and was also on the soccer team. Sarah, an English major, who was also a cheerleader, took a liking to the light skinned Ovu. She had assumed he was a black American until the day she said hello to him before the start of men's soccer practice. She had gone to the pitch to watch the practice. He had a heavy accent, and she asked where he was from and he told her. She was surprised to learn he was African, for she thought all Africans were dark skinned. She learned from Ovu that Africans came in different skin shades. He asked her out on a date and over time, they became very close friends. Ovu married her in his senior year of college.

Osak spent the rest of his Saturday perfecting a plan to take Felicia away to Africa for the circumcision and reincarnation rite on her. He had resisted long enough, but the threats his daughter faced from mysterious supernatural powers had to be addressed. His divided mind on whether these supernatural powers were real or not contributed to his earlier reticence to go along with what his parents had commanded him to do. Now his daughter was severely ill, and he feared for her life. But Felicia first had to improve to the point of being discharged from the hospital. He could then plan to take her out of the country for the circumcision before she got sick again.

Osak received additional ideas from Ovu in the course of the next week. Osak ultimately drew an elaborate plan consisting of seemingly difficult to execute objectives and tasks. The first part of the plan involved bringing his sister over from his country to stay with him and Ingrid. The purported purpose of that would be to help care for Felicia. This he would argue to Ingrid should help relieve them of the daily stress of having to drop off Felicia at her grandmother's and picking her back up again after work. It would also save them gas expenses. They still paid for the salary of the extra hand who replaced Eunice at the restaurant Eunice and Ronald owned so Eunice could look after Felicia in the day time. Eunice could go back to full time work again, saving them the salary of the extra hand. There were many benefits to having his sister around to care for Felicia, who continued to get better at the hospital and was nearing her discharge date.

Felicia came home after a month and a half stay at the Children's Hospital. She was slightly emaciated from all the drugs given to her, and the little food she ate as a consequence of her loss of appetite. But she showed signs of recovery because she moved her arms like babies did, whereas she had been quiet, not even crying, before her admission into the hospital. They were glad to have her back home; although Osak worried she could get sick again. His radical plan of action for a permanent remedy was stuck in his mind.

Osak was eating a late dinner with Ingrid one night when he decided to bring up the issue about his sister coming over from his country to stay with them. The traffic on the interstate had been particularly heavy going to pick up Felicia, then onwards home and they had arrived home later than usual.

"I have a suggestion to make, Ingrid."

"What is it?" Ingrid asked, looking up from her plate.

"I have thought about the stress we go through with caring for Felicia—taking her over to your mom in the morning and picking her up, and her general care in the home after work and on weekends. I thought I'd suggest that my younger sister come live with us and help us care for Felicia."

"How much do we have to pay her?" Ingrid asked.

"Nothing. She will live with us. We will only be responsible for her food, clothes, other necessities, and occasional gifts."

"That sounds like a good deal. Have you discussed this with her? Does she accept?"

"I have not, but I'm sure she will have no objection to it."

"Great! When is she coming?" Ingrid asked.

"As soon as I can arrange for her visa..."

"Ok," said Ingrid, nodding satisfactorily.

***

Zain, Osak's only sister, was 21 years old. She was dark skinned and tall like their father. She was curvaceous and walked with a sexy swing of her hips. She was also a third year college student studying child education. Student riots in the country had forced the authorities to shut down a number of institutions of higher learning and hers was among them. She had thus returned to her hometown to be with her parents until school was open again.

Zain helped to run a large supermarket in the town owned by her mother during the hiatus from school. Her phone rang one early morning as she supervised work at the supermarket, and it was Osak calling from the USA. She hadn't heard from him for several months. He sent her money every couple of months which sustained her on campus and called her three times per month, but he had cut off several months ago and the lack of contact had bothered her. She even tried calling him a number of times, but Osak's line had gone unanswered each time. Zain thought correctly that the issue with her brother's daughter in the USA had to have caused a family rift because Bilky, their mother, complained to her as well about Osak cutting off from her and King Ebu. Osak did continue sending Zain money for her upkeep in college, though. He just would not talk to any of them. When the phone had rung and it was Osak, Zain was excited and eager to talk to him again.

"Hi Osak, my beloved brother, how are you? I've been worried about you. You haven't called for a long time."

"Hello sister, I know it's been a while. I hope you're doing well."

"I am well. Mama and dad have been worried about you as well. They haven't heard from you in such a long while."

"I hope they are okay as well?" Osak asked.

"They have been worried so much about you and my little niece, Uwa. Please try and call them."

"I will do so."

Zain knew about the row between her brother and their parents, for she learned about most of it from their mother. She leaned to her brother's position on the issues, even though she did not express such to their mother. Perhaps because Zain and her brother were exposed to American culture and this made them progressive in their views and approach to life, she too thought that circumcision was outdated. She had herself been circumcised as a child, but she found it appalling that new parents in their town in "this modern age" still approved of the procedure on their girls. She was inclined to crusade against the practice, even starting out from her community, were it not for the fact that she was a princess and thus not expected to lead such a social protest movement.

The town, which was ruled by her dad, would be scandalized by such an act. She definitely saw the entire matter through the prism of her brother, but what she had been unaware of thus far was the mysterious and supernatural side of the whole matter, which had compelled Osak to change his mind on the issue, and had led to his phone call.

"I have good news for you," said Osak.

"I am excited," Zain replied.

"I want you to come and live with us and help my wife and me with the care of our daughter."

"Thank you Osak. This is a great opportunity for me. I've always wanted to live in America. Thank you again."

"I read in the media that your school was

closed over students' unrest. You will continue with your studies when you get here."

"Oh, thank you again. God bless you."

"I will soon send you the documents you will need to apply for an American visa. They should arrive within a week by courier service. Let me know when you receive them."

"Okay, I will do so once I receive them."

Zain was suffused with joy at the dramatic turn in her life's trajectory as a future resident of the USA. Like her brother, she loved America, and one of the things she prayed for was for a prospective husband who resided in America. Several men from the town, who lived in America, had returned home to marry local girls whom they took back to America to raise families with. Zain prayed and hoped to be fortunate to be betrothed in this way. Now, she would actually be going there as an unmarried woman, which was a better option than as a married person because in America she would have alternatives in the choice of a husband. She was happy, but she also hoped his brother would reconcile with their parents.

Osak called up King Ebu shortly after his conversation with Zain to inform him of his decision to bring her over to America. King Ebu was happy about that but he was also upset at his son for being out of touch for so long.

"Why did you stop calling us or take our calls?" King Ebu demanded to know.

Osak did not answer. He was calling from his office and had his father on a speaker phone.

"Are you still there?" King Ebu asked, slightly annoyed.

"I am, dad."

"You haven't answered my question...I can't say enough about the serious matters you have continued to ignore. I will warn you anew that you are endangering both yourself and your daughter. The oracle priest came to me several months ago to report an appearance by Uwa, and a threat from her to the effect that her reincarnate that was born in America would soon be recalled to the ancestral realm because her reincarnation rite had not been carried out more than a year after her birth. And that the child would be sickened as a warning before the return..."

Osak continued to listen intently to his father, but he was not the only listener. In the next office, Barbara had heard all that King Ebu said. It was fascinating to her, and she wondered whether Ingrid knew about what Barbara considered strange and crazy stuff she had heard on the call, and this wasn't the first time she had listened to what sounded like witch doctor stuff involving her boss.

King Ebu continued. "Your daughter will get sick, maybe she already has, I don't know, but know that you can get her out of her predicament if you comply as soon as possible with her circumcision and reincarnation rite."

Osak finally said something. "Dad, I am doing something about it, I won't go into any details now. I will keep you regularly informed as I make progress."

King Ebu had the last word. "Okay. Hurry up so Uwa won't return. We are honored to have her come back to our great family. Why do you want a black mark on your name as the one who made her decide not to stay? Please do not put such a dent on your name, reputation and our family. Again, please hurry up."

Osak turned off his phone following the conversation with his father to attend to his last late tax filing of the day. The lady had walked in exactly at the time of her appointment, just as Osak concluded his phone talk. From her adjoining office, Barbara processed check payments for mailing to clients.

Two hours later at about 6pm, Ingrid pulled up to the curb to pick up Osak for the routine journey to Ingrid's parents to pick up Felicia. Osak had not been by the curb as he had promised to be when Ingrid left her office across town. It was rush hour traffic and she couldn't park the vehicle without risking a fine and a tow by local traffic enforcement. She was thus compelled to sit in the car and wait, while watching out for traffic enforcement personnel. When Osak emerged several minutes later from his office across the street, a cop was writing Ingrid a citation for standing the vehicle in rush hour traffic. The fine was $100 and Ingrid was upset.

Ingrid wore a stern face when she drove off from the location after picking up Osak. He had caused her a traffic fine and she was unhappy about it. Ingrid's face showed displeasure, but Osak knew how to melt away her disapproving visage like hot knife through butter whenever he got into trouble with her. He tried to make her laugh.

"Do you know how the tortoise got its cracked shell?" he asked her, but she ignored the question because she still steamed from the traffic citation.

"Well, I will tell you the story from an African fable."

Ingrid was driving in rush hour traffic and pretended to ignore him, as he told the story.

"Tortoise, a cunning animal in African mythology, was invited to a feast somewhere in the sky. As he couldn't fly, he asked a bunch of birds to allow him to ride on their wings to the place in return for getting them into the feast. Well, they arrived there and Tortoise asked the birds to wait in an anteroom while he arranged to bring them food. He went into the dining hall where some of the best foods ever cooked were laid out on long tables. He sat at a table and was served extra portions of food, for he had claimed that he had guests with him. He alone ate all the food while the birds that brought him to the feast sat in the anteroom hungry. A bird spied into the dining hall and saw tortoise eating at a table, and the heaps of food on that table dwarfed him several times over. The birds knew at that point that they had been deceived by a greedy and fake friend, and they plotted revenge. On their way back to earth, with Tortoise riding on their wings, they suddenly broke up and dispersed, and

Tortoise hurtled from way up in the sky and crashed on the hard earth, shattering his hard shell.

It was a funny story which made her laugh.

"That was nice," she said.

CHAPTER 6

Felicia was now one year and five months old, and was fully recovered from her illness, although her doctor had warned of recurrences until she passed a certain age which he wasn't sure of when. The tax filing season was over and Osak's busiest work period of the year was now behind him. Ingrid suggested taking time off for a two-week vacation to the beaches of Florida. It was late spring again and the Florida beaches were really lovely places to visit. Ingrid had been fixated with them since her first college Spring Break trip to Florida. She recalled the wild parties and related activities staged by students from all over the country during Spring Break, but she was older now and had matured tastes. Her plan for herself, Osak and Felicia was a nice time out in a great hotel by the beach, where she and Osak would go for swims in the ocean, walks on the beach at night, dining at restaurants by the beach, and going for a short cruise on the ocean. Ingrid was certain they would return home after such great fun and quality time with each other fresh and rejuvenated.

Ingrid took about a week to make all the vacation arrangements, calling a hotel and making reservations, and booking airline and ocean cruise tickets. She was highly excited as she counted down to the day of their departure. The last time she and Osak, who was not really a vacation type guy, took time off to travel had been in the first year of their marriage. They had journeyed to the Ocean City Beaches which was but a three hour drive or so from their home. Osak, whose social exposure before his move to America had not featured anything that remotely resembled a vacation, was initially reluctant to go. He recalled that people who lived in the city/slum he resided in before his move to America were too harried and busy in an endless struggle to make ends meet to think about taking a vacation. The idea was a refined Western concept at a sharp variance with the realities of their grinding daily existence. He had ultimately given in to Ingrid's persuasion and went with her to Ocean City, where he thoroughly enjoyed himself for the one week they were there. He too was as excited as Ingrid was about their impending trip to Florida.

They took off for Florida from the Baltimore/Washington Airport on a bright sunny day. The 2 hour flight was smooth except for a couple of instances of turbulence mid way through the flight. They picked up a rental car at the Miami International Airport and drove to their hotel by the beach, arriving in the early evening. The plan was to relax by the hotel pool, eat dinner at the hotel restaurant, and catch a blues band performance in the hotel nightclub. The hotel ran a babysitter service, and this had been a primary selling point that made Ingrid make the reservation to stay there.

At about 8pm, Felicia was placed in the custody of the babysitter and they headed to the other side of the hotel for the blues concert. The ambience was relaxing and the soft blues music, which prominently featured melodious riffs from an electric guitar, was soothing to the senses. The wide glass windows of the nightclub enabled a nice view of the ocean and boats in the distance. Ingrid ordered steak and potatoes while Osak opted for mashed potatoes and gazpacho soup. They also ordered red wine and New York cheesecake for dessert.

Osak, in his seventh year of residency in America, was yet to be used to regular American food. His favorite food was still African food, especially the dish called *fufu* and soup. *Fufu* was mashed cassava or yam. The soup was made with vegetables, spices, dried shrimp or fish and either fresh fish or meat. The *fufu* was dipped in the soup and swallowed. This was the main traditional meal Osak had grown up on all his life. He had arrived in America to discover that he could not find the ingredients anywhere to make this meal, and he had lost weight over several months of eating very little of bland American food. This was during his college days. Years later, upon relocating to the Washington DC area in the state of Maryland, where international grocery stores existed, he was elated that he could now buy the ingredients to make his beloved *fufu* and thick soup.

The mashed potatoes and gazpacho soup (a soup made of green beans, chicken broth, tomato paste, diced tomatoes, pepper and onions) was the closest meal to *fufu* and thick soup. The candle light on the table, the view of the ocean through the transparent glass, the dimmed lights in the room, and the soft blues music made a perfect setting for the romantic dinner. The band struck up De Rabbit, an old Eric Gale number Osak was familiar with back home as a young man. It grabbed his attention and he left his chair to go sit somewhere closer to the band while it played the number. Ingrid was slightly amused at his reaction, but he told her it was a number he hadn't heard in more than 12 years, and he had to hear it again up close. It brought back good memories of his early teen years, first in his ancestral town then in the private Christian school his father enrolled him in, and later on the chaotic streets of the large city he lived in before his move to America. De Rabbit was a nice jazz number most radio stations played all the time.

The fun evening inside the nightclub lasted for about three hours. They left as more people entered the club. Felicia was asleep when they picked her up from the hotel babysitter. Osak carried her in his arms, as they walked to their room. Ingrid wanted to wake her up to feed her, but decided to let her sleep on until the next morning.

It was close to midnight when they went to bed. There were two beds in the room. Felicia was placed on the bed further inside the room. They took the second bed which was bigger. Within minutes of hitting the bed, Osak tried to make a move on Ingrid, grabbing her by the waist and pulling her closer. She laughingly pushed him off.

"The baby is here!" she protested.

"She is asleep! She is just a year old! It's okay!"

"No, it's not okay," she insisted, smiling in mild displeasure.

Osak was forced to suspend his amorous intent until another time. He recognized the situation with an impish smile and felt slightly embarrassed. There was a nightlight next to Felicia's bed. Ingrid left this light on so she could quickly reach out to her when she woke up. Ingrid then got under the covers and went to sleep.

***

Felicia woke up in the morning with a fever

and a cough. Ingrid had come with her medicines. She poured out a dose of fever medication which she gave to Felicia. Their morning plan was to stroll by the beach along with Felicia in her stroller. They would later drop her off at the hotel babysitter and return for a swim in the ocean, and a late lunch at a seafood restaurant. But Felicia's fever had put a hold on their plans. They watched her for the next couple of hours, hoping the fever would subside, but it didn't. It got worse, instead. They then decided as a precautionary measure, in case there was a deterioration, to take her to the hospital.

A half an hour later at the hospital, Felicia was seen by a pediatrician who diagnosed an ear infection and wrote a prescription for antibiotics. Minutes later, at the pharmacy, they filled the medicine and left to return to their hotel. Ingrid and Osak were worried for their daughter. They were disappointed that their vacation plans appeared headed to a truncation, but their daughter's health was paramount in their minds. If she mended quickly during the day, they hoped to get out and enjoy the sunny Florida weather.

The sun shone brightly in the sky, and a slight breeze blew from the blue ocean. It was a day to go swimming in the warm ocean waters, but Ingrid and Osak were forced to stay indoors in their hotel room to watch over Felicia, hoping she would get better. They watched movies and ordered room service. Felicia still ailed by the late evening, though her condition had slightly improved. The day was already gone, and so they decided to look forward to the next day. Felicia was bathed, fed, given her medicine and put to bed at about 8pm.

Felicia had continued to improve by the time she was put to bed, but the episode had flooded worries anew into Osak's mind. The whole circumcision and reincarnation stuff reared up again in his mind. Might this latest episode with Felicia be another manifestation of the effects of supernatural powers on her? The distressing state of mind he was suddenly plunged in made him decide to call Zain to follow up on her visa application, but he couldn't make the call in the presence of Ingrid. He told her he was going to the minimarket in the lobby to buy snacks, but in actuality, what he had told her was a cover so he could leave the room to speak privately to his sister.

Osak left the third floor room and walked to

the staircase where he took the stairs to the lobby of the hotel. He was in a hurry and did not want to wait for the elevators in the 20 floor hotel building. He couldn't spend too much time outside, lest he aroused suspicion. He couldn't also leave Ingrid for too long by herself with a sick baby. He needed to get outside the hotel for the quick call, come back into the lobby to pick up a couple of snacks, and head back up to the third floor. He was soon outside the hotel, and reached into his pocket to retrieve his phone.

Zain's phone rang loudly at about 3am local time in Africa. She had forgotten to mute the ring tone as she often did before retiring for the night. She was averse to being woken up by late night phone calls. Her hectic days working at her mother's supermarket left her exhausted. She thus hated late night calls that disturbed her sleep.

Zain woke up annoyingly to pick up the call, but she lightened up when she heard her brother's voice on the other end of the line.

"...I know it's the wee hours of the morning where you are right now. Sorry to wake you up!" said Osak.

"Good morning, my brother! How are you?"

"I am well, thank you!"

"How is Uwa doing?" Zain asked.

"She is fine. Thank you again...Zain, I wanted to find out whether you have submitted your application for a visa at the Embassy...I want you here as soon as possible."

"Yes, I have, and my interview is coming up next week," said Zain.

"That's lovely! Call me after your interview."

"Ok. I will do so."

"Ok. Good night, Zain."

Osak's phone call to his sister was short and to the point of why he had called her. He hurriedly came back into the hotel lobby and went to the minimarket where he picked up candy bars and potato chips.

Back upstairs, he went to where Felicia lay to check up on her. "How is she doing?" he asked Ingrid.

"I think she is doing much better," said Ingrid.

"I hope she keeps it up, so we can have some good fun outdoors tomorrow," said Ingrid, slightly optimistic.

"I sure hope so, too."

They munched on the snacks Osak brought

from the minimarket, cuddled up soon afterwards, and fell asleep. Felicia had been sleeping for about two hours by this time. Ingrid and Osak had closed their eyes for only about four hours when Felicia woke up crying, along with a coughing fit. Ingrid was the first to be woken up by her cries and she immediately picked her up. She tried to comfort her, as Osak, now awake, sat next to Ingrid and observed what was going on.

Ingrid was able to comfort her back to sleep again, but Ingrid and Osak would remain awake until the next morning, unable to fall asleep again. Ingrid recognized the situation as a case of their daughter just being ill again at the wrong time during a getaway they had looked forward to, but Osak believed supernatural powers were responsible, and his sister couldn't come over soon enough, so the second step in his plan to heal his daughter could start.

They took Felicia back to the pediatrician in the morning for reexamination. The young female doctor found that the ear infection was still there. It would take a few days for the medicine to have a full effect, but she also diagnosed Felicia with dehydration and prescribed a baby hydration formula. Felicia's health issues made them cut their two week vacation short, after only four days into it, and returned home.

CHAPTER 7

Zain was issued an American tourist visa on a day the US Embassy became a place for anguished crying because most people who had come for their visa interview were denied a visa. The unlucky applicants cried bitterly. America was the land flowing with the figurative milk and honey and many wanted to go there, but what many believed to be a visa quotas policy of the Embassy truncated their dreams. Zain had been lucky. Her lack of an international travel record, one of the predictors of a tourist returning to their home country upon expiration of their visa, put her in the category of the least qualified applicant to be issued a tourist visa, but she got it. She and Osak joked about it, after she had called him with the good news. Zain told him that Uwa supernaturally made it to happen.

Zain's visa was a single entry visa which would

expire in three months, though her brother had told her that she was likely to receive six months duration of stay approval at the airport upon her arrival. He intended to file for her change of visa status at a later time when she enrolled in college. Osak's stratagem to use her to accomplish something else was unknown to her at this point. Zain went home to prepare to leave the country. There were a number of things she had to get done before her departure.

Bilky made baby clothes Zain would take with her to America as gifts to her granddaughter. Zain took a few days to say her goodbyes to friends and relatives. Her schoolmates from college, all of whom were still at home from the school closures, were happy for her. At least she would restart college in America, whereas they were stuck in the country and forced to deal with perennial labor disputes between the government-owned institutions of higher learning and the academic staff unions. King Ebu and Bilky had a discussion with Zain on the night of the eve of her departure. They wanted to solicit her help in finding a way to nudge her brother to bring Felicia to them for her circumcision and ritual ceremony.

"Your brother has been in America only seven

years and he has decided to turn his back on our culture," said King Ebu. "He appears not to know that regardless of where any person from this town lives, our culture follows him. Then he is my designated successor, too."

"It maybe that his white wife is the one confusing him to refuse to do what our culture commands him to do," Said Bilky. "You must get close to him and make him remember home again."

Zain listened until they were finished talking. She thought her brother had every right to be left alone to decide how he wanted to live his life with his wife and daughter, but Zain was also a creature of the cultural milieu she and her brother grew up in where belief in superstition and the supernatural permeated life from birth till death. She thought her parents made some good points. Perhaps, her brother could be reasonable to meet them half way. He could agree to the reincarnation rite and oppose the circumcision. If Osak were to take this position, she decided she would support him. The discussions over, King Ebu told Zain he would pray for her at his traditional shrine. Zain was to take a bath and put on a white garment before the start of the session.

The next morning, about three hours before Zain hopped into a taxi that would take her to the airport for her flight, King Ebu took her to the back of his palace into a shrine to pray for her. King Ebu professed the Muslim faith, but he never totally jettisoned his traditional African religion which featured a bunch of gods which were intermediaries between Almighty God and humans. Each god had a carved wooden symbol that prayers were directed to. There were several carved symbols lined up against a wall inside the shrine. There were animal blood stains on the hard packed earth floor of the shrine, where sheep, goat and fowl had been sacrificed as offerings to the gods.

King Ebu ordered Zain to stand in front of the carvings, directly in front of a carving of a bearded man holding a machete. King Ebu stood beside Zain with a fowl in his right hand and began to utter incantations. He did this for 10 minutes then slaughtered the fowl. Blood spurts from the slit neck of the fowl hit the floor. King Ebu stepped forward and smeared blood on the carving depicting the bearded man. His eyes were red when he had finished, and he shook and sweated profusely. He seemed to have been momentarily transported spiritually somewhere, as he continued to tremble for another minute.

"Your journey will be a safe one, and our gods will be with you all the way on that plane that will take you there," he prayed. "You will get to America without any problems. All your wishes will be fulfilled there. You will be very important in bringing Uwa back. Amen!" King Ebu poured a little bit of gin libation on the floor of the shrine, and on the carving with the bearded man.

"It is done," he said to Zain, and they left the shrine.

Zain had always felt uneasy about the fetish practices of her father. Why was he doing that while he was still a Muslim? The Islamic religion of Muslims did not recognize pagan gods. It was a monotheistic religion which believed in Allah (The Almighty God) and Muhammad as his messenger. These pagan gods represented by carvings he lined up in a shrine had no powers to do anything. Zain had once asked her father why he did such things, and King Ebu had responded by telling Zain that his traditional religion had existed before Islam came into their lives centuries ago. He was Muslim quite okay, but as the king of the town and the custodian of its culture, he was invariably obligated to worship these gods. He had also read the bible, and he pointed out to his daughter the passage in the bible where even Jesus said one should give to Caesar what belonged to him, and to God what belonged to God. There was therefore nothing wrong with his dual religion.

Far away in the USA, at the same time that the activity was going on inside the shrine, Osak and Ingrid were driving to work after dropping off Felicia with Eunice. Zain was to arrive in the morning of the next day after an all night flight from Africa to Washington National Airport. Osak was to pick her up. Ingrid had wanted to come, but Osak persuaded her not to come. He feared his sister would unwittingly reveal information to innocent questions Ingrid might ask in the course of the drive to and from the airport. Ingrid did not think anything of his insistence to go alone to the airport to pick up Zain.

Later in the day at his office, Osak thought about his sister's impending arrival, which would mark a successful execution of the first stage of his plan to take Felicia with him to Africa. The remaining stages of the plan were complicated and risky but he was determined to see them through. He didn't accomplish much work because he was consumed by what he planned to do. There was a high risk of the consequences of a failure being Ingrid filing for divorce, and he was troubled by it because he loved Ingrid dearly. He had come close to telling Ingrid a couple of times everything about what his parents wanted him to do, and to explain to her that they were necessary to stop Felicia's intermittent illness, and even prevent her premature death, but he wasn't sure that Ingrid would buy it. And should that be the case, she would forever never trust him with Felicia.

Across town in Ingrid's office, she told her close friends about her sister in law, en route to the USA to stay with Ingrid and her husband and daughter. She was excited about it. Sharon, a new employee at the company and one of Ingrid's friends, appeared not too enthused for her friend. She asked to speak with Ingrid when she had a few moments.

"I have something I want to share with you," said Sharon.

"What is it?"

"When you have a few moments, we can talk. Is that okay?"

"Sure, we can! Let's do it after lunch," said Ingrid.

"Okay, that's fine."

Sharon was a tall skinny blonde. She had a round face with high cheek bones, full lips and light brown eyes. She and Ingrid had many things in common. They married foreign men, although Sharon's marriage had ended after three years; they both had Scandinavian ancestry; they were born in the same month; and both of their grandfathers had served in the Second World War. They shared a couple of contrasts, as well—Ingrid was affable and socially comfortable, whereas Sharon was an introvert and inscrutable. But Ingrid understood her better the more they came to know each other.

There was much work around the office. Ingrid had just left one of the law partner's offices, much later in the day, when she noticed Sharon walking towards the main double doors which opened into the street outside. She figured Sharon was going outside the building for a smoke, a habit she had been working on her friend to quit. Ingrid figured this was the best time to hear what Sharon wanted to share with her earlier, and so she followed her. The traffic flow on the street outside was typical of midday Washington DC, slightly heavy with one or two impatient taxis driving through red lights. The sidewalks were full of people—delivery drivers, mailmen, hot food stands with lines of people waiting to buy food, and people generally walking up and down to various destinations. Sharon had company in a number of fellow smokers from the building and adjoining buildings who were outside on smoke breaks. She had lit up her cigarette when she noticed Ingrid push open the double doors and step outside.

"... I know, I know," Sharon said defensively. "It's my smoking habit, right! Okay, this is my last smoke and I will quit."

Ingrid had heard those words from her friend many times before without Sharon actually summoning the required will and discipline to do it. But Sharon's smoking was not the reason Ingrid had followed her outside.

"I know you can do it," she said, still encouraging her friend.

"...But that's not an issue today. I will cut you a break. I will not harangue you today," Ingrid joked. "What is it that you wanted to share with me from earlier on?" she asked.

Sharon drew a long smoke from the thin cigarette she held between her fore and middle fingers then blew out the smoke through her thin lips. Her deep red lip stick made a circular mark on the brown cigarette filter. Specks of ash were blown by the wind onto her black and white striped business suit. She took another long draw from the cigarette, exhaled the smoke then threw the half smoked cigarette away. She did not want to offend Ingrid by blowing cigarette smoke onto her face as they talked.

"Well, Ingrid my dear friend, I heard you express excitement about your sister-in-law coming from Africa to join your husband and you," said Sharon. "...And I wanted to help you to make sure that no surprises were sprung up on you."

"What do you mean?" Ingrid asked, confused at what her friend had just said.

"Are you sure this sister-in-law is not your husband's African wife?" Sharon asked.

"Sharon, don't be silly!" Ingrid playfully admonished, laughing.

"I am serious, Ingrid. Maybe you don't know that their cultures and laws allow them to marry multiple wives over there, and they come here to marry American wives without telling them about their African family."

"Sharon, Osak has no other wife but me,"

Ingrid insisted.

Sharon's broken marriage had been caused by a bigamous relationship her North African husband had going without her knowledge. Samir, her husband, had been married in his teens to a lady through an arranged marriage process, a practice common in the society he grew up in. Sharon had met him in college in the Midwest where he was pursuing a graduate degree. Samir was a graduate assistant and taught a statistics class Sharon was enrolled in. He liked her but refrained from making any romantic moves on her until the semester was over. Then he asked her out to dinner one night, took her to his apartment and treated her very nicely. They dated for six months before he proposed marriage to her. As Samir was asking Sharon's hand in marriage in America, four thousand miles away in an arid village somewhere in North Africa, his African wife, a woman named Salma, and their seven year old son lived in Samir's village home, where Salma ran a local restaurant. Samir turned out not to be effectively discreet in his dealings with his other family. Sharon's suspicions of Samir's calls, financial transactions and email activities had busted up his secret. Deeply hurt, she filed for divorce. They had only been married for one year.

Sharon narrated her emotional story to Ingrid.

"...I was deeply hurt. I don't want you to get hurt like I was," she told Ingrid. "That's the reason for telling you about my experience. Make sure this lady is who she says she is."

"But how can I verify her identity?" Ingrid protested. She didn't think it was logical for Osak to bring an 'African wife' to live with them, assuming he had one. Wouldn't he try to hide her, like Sharon's husband had tried to hide his, she reasoned.

"It wouldn't make any sense for Osak to bring another 'wife' into our household, if he had one" she told Sharon. "He is educated. He knows it is bigamy and it is a crime. I don't think he is capable of a despicable act like that," Ingrid continued in a forceful vouch for her husband's integrity.

"I am only looking out for your best interests," said Sharon.

Ingrid did not know what to make of Sharon's unusual counsel. There certainly was an element of concern in her, but the whole episode had also appeared surreal. She thought Sharon's dive into bigamy, a lying husband, and how she snooped into his affairs to expose him were all stuff of gossip tabloids, totally non applicable to her marriage. She still decided to thank her for her concern.

"Sharon, you are a really good person for your concern for me. Your story was really crazy. I have never ever heard of a wild story like that before."

"These things do happen," said Sharon. "How about this other story of a guy from this Asian country who took his American wife on a visit to his country and decided they were not coming back to America. His wife opposed the idea and wanted to come back, but he locked her up in a room for two years before law enforcement found out and freed her."

"What!" Ingrid exclaimed.

Ingrid felt empathy towards Sharon, but she also thought Sharon had been unlucky to have met a deceitful man, something her own Osak was definitely a contrast with. She had known him for about five years and lived with him for four years now, a time period more than enough to learn about a partner's personality and their behaviors. There was just no way could Osak be placed in the same category of liars as Samir and the man who locked his wife away for two years.

CHAPTER 8

Zain arrived at the Baltimore/Washington International Airport on a Saturday morning on a flight from Africa. It was an eleven hour flight buffeted by so much turbulence as the plane sliced through the icy air. Zain was flying international for the first time, and the flight had been too long for her. The turbulence and its associated anxiety tightened up her stomach and killed her appetite. She had been uncomfortable throughout the flight, which couldn't have arrived soon enough at the time that it did. She went through immigration and customs and soon was walking towards the sliding doors that opened to the access road outside.

Osak had come with Felicia who was strapped in her car seat. She was sprightly dressed up in colorful baby's overalls, and her straight brown hair was bunched up in a pony. Felicia took after her mother much more than Osak in physical appearance. She was highly light skinned and straight haired. She also had her mother's oblong shaped face and pointed nose.

Osak had stood next to the vehicle, as he waited for his sister to exit the airport terminal. He dared not leave the vehicle unattended to go into the terminal to look for her, lest airport police issue him a citation and impound the vehicle. As he had already told Zain what to do in a phone call with her just before she left Africa—to walk out of the terminal onto the access road—he hoped she would do just that.

Osak had waited anxiously for about ten minutes before observing her walk through the doors onto the pavement adjacent to the roadway. He strode up a few yards to meet her. They smiled and embraced joyously. The last they had seen each other had been seven long years ago. Osak carried her luggage for the short walk to his vehicle. They were out of the airport vicinity within minutes, as Osak pulled the vehicle into traffic. Osak had asked Zain to sit in the front passenger seat, but Zain was super excited to see her little niece. She elected to sit in the back and be near Felicia.

Zain stared at Felicia in amazement. This was

her first time seeing a mixed race baby and this baby was part of her, as a half offspring of the Ebu family. She was fascinated with Felicia's physical appearance. She attempted to take Felicia out of her car seat so she could carry her in her arms, but Osak stopped her for reasons of safety and to avoid a citation from a traffic officer for failure to secure a baby in a car seat as required by law. He had to explain the law to Zain, who was jocularly insistent on carrying her niece in her arms.

"...Don't worry Zain," he assured her. "You will get to carry her in your arms plenty of times any time you want. Just let us get home first."

"How are our parents? I hope they were fine when you left home yesterday," he inquired.

"They are well," said Zain.

"What about our hometown and the country in general? Are the institutions of higher learning still shut because of the strike?"

"Our hometown is fine. Dad has everything under control. It's just that he has created a buzz about an impending big ceremony to welcome the reincarnated matriarch of the town in your daughter..."

Osak bit his lower lip after hearing what Zain had just said. He had not bought into this superstition in the beginning, but as Felicia ailed every now and then, and came close to death on a couple of occasions, he became sold on the destiny of his daughter being tied to supernatural powers that could wreak havoc with that destiny if he failed to carry out the activities he was told would release the hold of the supernatural powers. He had decided he would do it, and how he would do it was majorly the reason why Zain was now around, although Zain did not know it just yet. The enormity of the challenge involved in successfully carrying out his plans weighed on him. Zain's mention of the ceremony was thus an immediate stressor which made his heart to skip a beat.

"Did dad tell you when this ceremony will hold?" he asked her.

"Dad said it will hold only when Uwa is brought back to the community for the ceremony which will also involve ritual activities," replied Zain, who called Felicia by her supposed original name from her first lifetime on earth.

Osak paused for a long while until Zain broke the silence.

"You will have to travel home with Uwa for the ceremony," she stated.

If only Zain knew how complicated it was to do what she had just stated, Osak thought for a moment. If only she knew that his white wife would brook no such thing, and might even file for divorce, as a consequence of even trying to persuade her to go along. If only Zain knew that getting Felicia into Africa for this ceremony and associated circumcision was easier said than done, perfectly akin to a popular proverb in their language that associated the impossible with dogs growing horns someday, perhaps she wouldn't have made her statement in the perfunctory manner that she did. In any case, Zain was now here in America and she was a critical component in the plot he cooked that would see Felicia taken to the African continent. He did not plan to let her know just yet of the role she would play until the appropriate time, a few months into the future.

Zain played with Felicia, as Osak navigated the light Saturday morning traffic, driving slightly below the speed limit. Zain pulled Felicia's little hands lightly and tickled her. Felicia smiled at Zain in excitement. Zain touched her hair and felt its smooth texture. She never stopped marveling at her little niece, and her eyes remained fixated on Felicia as she conversed with Osak.

"I am looking forward to meeting your wife," said Zain.

"She as well," said Osak. "You will like my wife. She is a very nice person, and the best thing that ever happened to me."

"Is she the type that will agree to relocate with you, should you decide to return to Africa?" Zain asked.

Well, we haven't had that conversation yet, but I am not thinking about relocation anytime soon."

"I asked because you are the heir to the throne of our hometown. Should anything happen to dad, you are the next king. Won't you relocate to take up the kingship?"

"I haven't thought about all of that yet. I wish dad great health such that he continues as king for many more decades."

"I have the same wish for dad as you do, but you can't rule out anything unexpected happening which could thrust the kingship on you," Zain admonished.

"Zain, my beloved sister, I heard you loud and clear, I will cross that bridge when I get to it."

Osak avoided hitting a deer as he pulled into his street. The animals often foraged in the bushes on the edges of the estate, and were known to roam the quiet streets. Zain had been momentarily agitated when she saw the beast. Her shock was attributed to the fact that she had never seen one before. She had read about wild animals like the deer she had just seen in her geography books in high school and thought they existed only in Africa. There were animals in her community back home, but they were all domesticated animals—goats, sheep, pigs, and cattle. Unlike the East African bushes where lions, antelope and the like thrived, the West African region where her hometown was located in did not have many wild animals.

"What was that?" she asked Osak with a start, straining her neck to look at the large male deer which galloped towards the bushes.

"It's a deer," said Osak. "We have so many of them around here."

"They come here in this built up estate?" she asked incredulously.

"We have bushes around here that they graze in."

"People living in this estate are very lucky then," she said. "They have plenty of meat to eat."

"No, the animals cannot be hunted like that. It's against the law. Only the government decides when they can be hunted," said Osak.

"You mean no one can spear the beast that I just saw and kill it? What sort of nonsense law is that," mocked Jane of the law. "I wish we had deer like this in our hometown. No government can save them." They both laughed at the joke.

"We must be getting close to your house," said Zain.

"Yes, we will arrive there shortly."

Osak soon pulled up to the front of his house and pressed on the horn for Ingrid's attention. She looked through a window to observe his car and she stepped outside. Zain alighted from the vehicle. Osak came around to remove her luggage from the trunk then picked up Felicia. They walked up to Ingrid who was wearing a white top and blue jeans, and stood on the porch.

She stretched out her right hand to shake Zain's hands then hugged her briefly.

"Welcome to our home."

"Thank you," said Zain.

"How was your flight?"

"It was okay," said Zain, who elected not to bother telling Ingrid about how awful the turbulence-hit flight had been. Zain figured she would have to go into the details about her experience, and she didn't think it was appropriate to do so in her first conversational encounter with her sister in law, whom she was setting eyes on for the first time. It was better, in her opinion, for her first extended conversation with Ingrid to be on something happy and cheerful in nature.

The welcome pleasantries on the porch lasted for a couple of minutes before Osak handed over Felicia to Ingrid, picked up Zain's luggage, and pushed open the front door. Inside the well furnished home, Zain marveled at the opulence. Ingrid wanted to show her around the house, but she had been cooking lunch during the period Osak and Felicia had been out to the airport to pick up Zain. She wanted to serve this lunch before showing Zain around the house.

Zain sat in the living room where Osak had switched the television on for her. Ingrid walked back and forth between the kitchen and the dining room, as she put out the dishes she had made to fete her sister in law with. She had made lasagna, baked chicken, mashed potatoes, gazpacho soup (her husband's favorite), rolls, carrot cake, a salad of mixed veggies (romaine lettuce, water cress, carrots and onions), and spiced oxtail. Osak had taught her how to make oxtail, an African delicacy Ingrid had never heard of until Osak brought the meat home one day and cooked it. She did not eat it the first few times Osak cooked the delicacy. She thought the tail of cattle was typically thrown away by meat packing companies or used in making dog food, and so she refused to eat it. But the kind of loving relationship she had with Osak was such that she didn't mind bending to his predilections if they were not outrageous and extreme, and trying some kind of strange meat he liked to eat was not an extreme act. So, she tried it one day and it didn't taste badly.

Ingrid invited Zain to the dining room table when she was ready. They waited for Osak, who was briefly in his home office in the basement, to join them. They conversed as they waited.

"That's a lot of food," Zain exclaimed. "The dishes look very appetizing."

"Thank you," said Ingrid. "I hope you'll like them."

The noise of Osak's footsteps on the basement stairs wafted up to the hearing of the women, who were ready to start eating, but hesitated until he took his seat. Finally taking his seat, he said the before-meal prayer after which they dove into the food. Osak went for the gazpacho and the mashed potatoes, his replacement meal for the *fufu* and thick African vegetable/meat/fish soup he grew up on in Africa. He had started to make oxtail and thick African soup about twice a month, but making them was time consuming. Ingrid made oxtail too but she cooked them only on special occasions such as this one today to welcome Zain. As Zain was now here, Osak hoped his beloved thick African soup would be regular fare in the house.

Zain tried the lasagna, even though she'd never eaten any before, and liked it. She also ate some of the salad. Osak was amazed at his sister's ease in consuming American food. He was in his seventh year of American residency, yet he was yet to acquire a taste for lasagna. He had once despised salad, but was persuaded by Ingrid to start eating it because it was healthy food. One of his tasks in his boyhood years back home was to put out the family's goats and sheep to pasture in the surrounding bushes where the animals munched on green vegetation. The greens of his hometown bushes had a resemblance to the salads he saw in America, and he had formed a psychological block in his brain never to eat them. When Ingrid noticed that he didn't like salads and she asked why, he told her salads were goat food. She had thought he was being silly, but she later realized she had to work on him to change his mind set about salads.

"How did you acquire the taste for American food?" he asked Zain.

Zain laughed. "Food is like music," she answered. "It is a universal thing. The cultural background of the food does not matter."

"You live in America. Don't you like American foods?" she asked him.

"Some American foods I do like, but it took me some time to get used to them."

Ingrid had to chime in. "Zain, don't listen to him," she said in jest. "Enjoy your food."

CHAPTER 9

Felicia was 20 months old when she fell seriously ill again. Zain had been with the family for only three months when the incident had occurred. She had been babysitting her since her arrival and had developed a close relationship with Ingrid during this period. The trust so created gave Ingrid the confidence of leaving Felicia in Zain's care during her working hours. Ingrid was initially skeptical about doing that, even though the main reason Zain had come to stay with them, Osak had told her, was so she would help with Felicia's care. It was a great relief to have Zain around taking care of Felicia. Not only that, but she also cooked and cleaned the house. Ingrid thus found the time to do a number of things she had always wanted to do, but couldn't because of her tight daily schedule. She found time to enroll in an aerobics class, and she restarted her law school entrance examination classes. It was all going well until this latest episode of Felicia's illness.

Osak and Ingrid had left for work in the morning of that day. Felicia was still asleep when they had left. Zain folded clothes in the laundry room and was about thirty minutes into this activity when she heard Felicia's cries. She had woken up. Zain hurried upstairs to check on her. When she picked Felicia up, Zain noticed that she was running a temperature, for her body was hot. She had also vomited and her diaper was full with watery stool.

Zain called Ingrid to alert her of the situation, and Ingrid directed her to the medicine cabinet where Felicia's medications were stored. Ingrid told her the types and the dosage to give to Felicia. Zain stayed on the phone with Ingrid for several minutes, as Ingrid asked several questions about Felicia's condition—whether she had been fed, given a bath, and what her temperature was. They hung up, at which point Zain went to the medicine cabinet where she retrieved Felicia's medications. She administered the medicines as had been directed by Ingrid and thereafter gave Felicia a bath. When she attempted to feed her, she showed no interest then she vomited for the second time. Zain cradled and rocked her gently to make her sleep. She did this for about thirty minutes and got her to go to sleep. Zain laid her back in her bed and went back downstairs to continue with folding clothes.

Zain was worried for Felicia as she folded clothes—a pair of pants now, then a dress, Osak's shirts, and Felicia's small sized clothes. She did the family laundry once a week. Along with cleaning and babysitting Felicia, these activities kept her busy in an otherwise new life of involuntary isolation in the high-end estate her brother and his wife lived in. Back home in Africa, neighbors mingled freely and made unannounced visits to each other's home. People sat on their porches and exchanged impromptu pleasantries with people walking by. But in this new American neighborhood she now called home, there was none of the social dynamics she was used to. She looked out the living room window into the street on some days and not a single soul could be seen walking on the street. Every home looked like an island onto itself, and there was no social interaction of any kind among the residents of the estate. Her initial boredom which lasted for about a week, which Ingrid had partially contributed to unintentionally because she continued dropping off Felicia with Eunice, was broken when she started taking full time care of Felicia. She adored Felicia and cared for her like her own child. She was thus very worried about Felicia's sudden illness. Zain went back upstairs to check on her.

Felicia was still asleep. Zain reached out and touched her forehead. It still blazed hot with a fever. She also noticed a slight tremor in her. At that moment, her phone rang, and it was Ingrid calling.

"Hello Zain, how is Felicia feeling?"

"I am with her now," said Zain. "She is asleep but is still running a very high fever."

"I am leaving work right now," said Ingrid with a hint of stress in her voice. "She needs to see a doctor. I'll see you soon."

Ingrid called Osak to alert him of the latest update on Felicia's condition. She had called him earlier after her initial conversation with Zain. They had both hoped that the medications Zain was instructed to give her would stop the fever. But their hopes did not materialize, and Ingrid had decided to leave work to take her to the hospital.

"I'm on my way home now," she told him.

"Okay. Call me from the hospital when you arrive, and after seeing the doctor," he asked of her.

"I will do so."

Ingrid drove through short cuts in the city to get to the highway leading out of Washington DC into Maryland. She wanted to get to her sick daughter as quickly as possible. She came close to driving through two red lights in her haste. Finally on the highway, she passed a speed enforcement camera device mounted beside the highway. The camera flashed and she knew she had been snapped driving beyond the speed limit of 45 miles per hour. The citation will arrive in the mail and will probably carry a $100 fine, but she was not worried about that right now as she sped on. She arrived home in record time, but before she turned into her street, she placed a call to Zain on her mobile phone.

"Zain, I will be arriving home in minutes. How is Felicia doing? Please dress her up for me to take her to the hospital."

"Okay, I will do so right away," Zain replied.

Ingrid parked the car in front of the house and fast walked into the house. Zain held Felicia in her arms, as Ingrid walked in. Zain handed her Felicia, who now looked pale. Ingrid kissed her cheeks and felt her forehead and the rest of her body.

"Zain, we are leaving immediately for the hospital, me and Felicia."

"Can I come?" Zain asked.

"Yes, you can," said Ingrid.

They were inside Ingrid's car within minutes. After strapping Felicia in her car seat, Ingrid started up the vehicle and drove off, en route to Children's Hospital.

In his office, the matter of Felicia's latest ill health bothered Osak. It must be those supernatural powers again, he reasoned, and it was necessary for him to hurry up with his plan to get Felicia to Africa where these supernatural powers would be appeased so his daughter would get a new lease on life. He was at times still ambivalent about these mysterious issues raised by his parents, but every now and then, he would have these dreams that entrenched the supernatural hold in his mind, as had occurred the previous night.

The same nine feet tall, old and wrinkled woman had showed up again in the dream. She had issued him a final warning about the reincarnation rite and gave him six months to get it done or she would return to the spirit realm of the ancestors. He was alarmed when he woke up, but as he prepared to leave for work, Felicia was fine. There was nothing out of the ordinary going on with her. He had even carried her briefly and tickled her to laugh. It had therefore been extremely disconcerting to him when Ingrid called to alert him of Felicia's health crisis later in the day. That wrinkled woman who was issuing him these warnings through dreams certainly meant business, but at least she had given him six months to comply. That was enough time, he thought. What he needed to do now was to get on with putting the next piece of his plan together, and this had to do with his hometown association. It had a scheduled meeting during the coming weekend, about a day away, and he planned to be present.

The association had members living throughout the USA. It had annual conventions during which members and their families gathered to deliberate about development projects for their common ancestral hometown, made decisions on projects and funding (usually through a general levy of members) and got some recreation and relaxation. These conventions lasted over a weekend, and they were rotationally held in the West Coast, East Coast, and the Midwest. The previous year's convention had been held in the East Coast in New York City. The current year's convention was supposed to hold in the West Coast in Los Angeles.

The coming weekend's scheduled meeting was to discuss and approve the agenda and hosting costs for the Los Angeles convention. Osak had other ideas about that, and it was associated with his plans to get Felicia to Africa. He needed the support of Ovu, his confidante, for something he intended to do at the meeting. He decided to call him later to ask for that support. Osak's plan was to move a motion to have the convention held in the East Coast for the second year in a row, and he wanted it held in New York. He would find a way to persuade Ingrid not to come with him, but he would take Felicia with him to the convention. Ingrid would probably be concerned about proper care for Felicia, but he would tell her that Zain, who would come along, would take care of that as her babysitter. But before all of this could happen, he had to secure the vote of the association to do something it had never done before, and it was to hold a convention in the same zone of the USA for two consecutive years. Still bothered by Felicia's health situation, which had just flashed through his mind, he picked up his phone and called Ingrid. It rang a few times before Ingrid picked up. It had been about 40 minutes since their last conversation.

"Hello!"

"What is the situation now?" he asked. "We arrived about 20 minutes ago," said Ingrid. "We are now with the doctor, who is now running a series of tests."

"Okay. Call me back with further developments."

"I will do so," said Ingrid. "Bye! Talk to you later"

Felicia was treated and kept for several hours so her health could be monitored. She slowly recovered during this period and by 11pm, was well enough to be discharged. Ingrid and Zain were in the hospital throughout that time, waiting anxiously and praying. Felicia was much better when Ingrid picked her up out of her hospital bed. The fever was gone, and her eyes were clear and bright again. She had just been fed by a nurse and she burped a couple of times. Soon, they were headed for home, and arrived slightly before midnight.

Ingrid stepped into the house, totally exhausted. She had been away at the hospital for eleven hours. She wanted to go to sleep, but Osak had made a late dinner of pasta and chicken. Late night meals were a problem for her because it gave her indigestion, but she was also hungry, having skipped lunch to get home quickly to take Felicia to the hospital. She ate half of the food, took a shower and retired for the night.

Osak had planned to stay awake for another hour, as he planned to call Ovu. As soon as Ingrid had gone to bed, Osak went downstairs to his basement office to make the call. Ovu was asleep, for it was close to 1am when his phone had rung. His wife, who lay beside him, was woken up by the ring. As usual she suspected it was Osak, for she had come to mark him with the notoriety of making late night calls to Ovu.

"Ovu, my brother, I am sorry once again to be making another late night call to you," said Osak. "Are you alone?" he asked.

"No, what's going on?" Ovu asked.

"Can I get 5 minutes of your private time, if you don't mind?" Osak asked.

"Yes, no problem at all about that," Ovu

obliged.

Ovu got out of bed to his wife's chagrin and headed out the bedroom door to the stairs that led to the living room. He turned on the television to mask his voice in the course of the discussion with his friend.

"I'm good now Osak, what's going on?"

"My apologies once again for the late night call," said Osak. "As you know, the association meeting is tomorrow Saturday, and I want your support in a motion I want to move to repeat our annual convention here in the east coast this year in New York."

"Why, what's the purpose for that?" Ovu asked.

"You already know about this my matter regarding my daughter. I have perfected the plan you and I started sometime ago to take her to Africa, and the only way I can do this is to use the 4-day window of our annual convention to fly out with her for the ceremonies and circumcision in Africa, and get back to America. I know by rotation, our annual convention is supposed to rotate out to the West Coast in Los Angeles, but flying out to LA and then back across the country and out to Africa will cause me to lose days from the 4-day window I need to get this done and get back. I must fly out of a nearby airport and JFK is the ideal airport."

"Your plan is quite daring," said Ovu. "You can still buy your ticket to leave out of New York on the weekend of the convention. The LA location of the convention should not have anything to do with where you leave from, I think."

"Ovu, I must do this with minimal suspicion by Ingrid. Mind you, she will not be traveling with me. I can persuade her not to come, that I am taking Felicia with me to introduce her to her uncles and aunts from our community scattered all over America. I cannot tell her I'm traveling to LA only for her to find out that I had planned to travel to New York all along."

"How will she find out unless you tell her," said Ovu.

"It is true, but I don't want to take any chances at all on that. Anything can happen. A call can come to her, for instance without my knowledge for whatever reason, from the travel agency or airline about my presence in New York, were I to inform her about going to LA for our convention. And I can't lie to her about the convention holding in New York, when it's in fact in LA because, again, something can happen at that convention. A fight could break out; somebody could get hurt which could warrant a TV report about it. You can imagine a screaming headline stating: 'Several People Injured At An African Convention in LA,' and Ingrid seeing that on the news to find out that the location I had told her that the convention would hold in (i.e. New York) was a lie."

"Ok, I see your point now," said Ovu.

"I need to be as efficiently deceptive about this as I can be, get to Africa for the things that need to be done for my daughter, and get back here in 4 days. I must therefore move this motion to hold the convention in New York, buy my tickets from Washington to New York, and New York to Africa and back to New York."

"What a well thought out plan!" said Ovu, in astonishment. "I will support the motion. There will likely be opponents, particularly from association members residing on the West Coast who won't like their turn to host being taken away from them, but we will press the matter and apply the necessary pressure."

"You will have to do some lobbying before the meeting tomorrow," said Osak.

"I will do so for you tomorrow morning," Ovu promised.

"Okay. Thank you. I'm very grateful."

"You're welcome! Goodnight."

It was 2am when Osak came upstairs from the basement to climb in bed beside Ingrid. Zain was fast asleep and Felicia was having a good night rest as well. She had retained her food, stopped vomiting and was sound asleep. Osak tossed and turned throughout the night, unable to sleep. What he was embarked upon was a betrayal of Ingrid, a woman he loved so dearly. It was unfortunate, he thought, that she wouldn't understand why it was necessary for him to do it. Their cultural differences could never be bridged here. He had flirted a few times with telling her about it, hoping he'd be able to convince her, but each time he thought so, his instincts got the better of him about her never ever agreeing to a circumcision of Felicia. She might agree to the reincarnation rite, considering no bodily scarring of Felicia would be involved, but she was most likely to draw the line on circumcision.

CHAPTER 10

The association met as scheduled to discuss its forthcoming convention. Ovu had lobbied heavily for support of Osak's motion as he had promised. In the course of the marathon meeting, which was held by teleconference, Osak's motion was introduced and it narrowly passed. The convention would be moved to New York City from Los Angeles, which had been chosen at the close of the previous year's convention in New York. There were a few West Coast residents on the call who were not pleased with the vote, and they threatened a boycott of the convention. But Ovu had done a masterful job in corralling the votes for Osak, arguing that the association's planned fundraiser at the convention was likely to raise bigger money in the East Coast where 60% of the association's members resided in. They had a lot of friends who would likely attend as friends of the association. Unbeknownst to the association's members, the change of venue was actually in connection with an elaborate plan concocted by Osak, aided by Ovu.

Osak's second leg of his plan was now in place. The third leg involved finding a way to get Ingrid into agreeing not to travel with him to the convention, and to agree with him to take Felicia along for the purposes of showing her off to his kinsfolk. The convention was about a couple of months away in the summer, about the same period Ingrid wanted to take her law school entrance examinations. He knew she would need some quiet time to study for the notoriously difficult examinations required for admission into law schools. Ingrid had set her sights at being admitted into a top law school. Osak bide his time until a quiet weekend moment, when they particularly enjoyed each other's company with a home movie, wine and popcorn. He would raise the convention and law school examination matters for a discussion.

The moment arrived a month before the July convention and Ingrid's examinations, which was to hold a week after the convention.

"You most definitely need some quiet time to study for the examinations," he told her. "I will take Felicia along with me."

"Can you handle her well?" she asked. "I don't see how you can do it and be a part of the convention activities."

"Zain can come with us to help care for her," he suggested.

"Have you spoken to her about it?" she asked.

"I have not, but I don't think she will object."

"Okay, as long as Zain agrees to it, I'm fine with it, but I will also talk to her," she said. "Where is the convention holding?"

"In New York City."

"That's not that far," said Ingrid. "It shouldn't physically affect Felicia that much. You can even drive there."

"I think it's better to fly," said Osak.

Ingrid was glad to have the free undisturbed time she needed to study for the examinations. Her law school ambition had been temporarily suspended due to her marriage and childbirth. She had always wanted to become a lawyer, and so passing her examinations to get into law school was very important to her. If only she knew that the man who was her heartthrob was actually planning a trip to New York ostensibly for a convention, but in actuality was going overseas to Africa for a circumcision and a pagan ritual ceremony with her daughter in the middle of it. The third leg of Osak's plan was now in place. He now had to execute the fourth and final part, which was the most risky and dangerous.

***

Felicia, being less than 2 years of age, could either travel under her own passport or as an endorsee in the passport of either of her parents. Osak elected to procure a passport and a visa for her. He contacted a travel agent and paid the necessary fees to get them done. Two weeks before his planned departure, he called his parents to notify them of his impending trip with Felicia. He had made the call from his office, for he dared not do it from home. He had a four day window to do all that needed to be done to Felicia, and so he wanted them to prepare to accommodate his time frame.

King Ebu was eating a heavy meal of *fufu* and thick fish and vegetable soup when his phone had rang. It was mid afternoon when the African rainy season was especially hot and humid. He sweated as he put big balls of the *fufu,* dipped in the thick soup, in his mouth and swallowed. He picked up the phone to answer. His son's voice brought a beam to his face.

"Hello Osak, how are you?"

Bilky was at the back of the house, and King Ebu shouted out her name to come join him in the room, as Osak was on the phone from America. He turned on the speaker feature on the phone so Bilky could hear Osak.

"I am well," Osak answered. "How is mama?"

"Your mother is fine."

There was a long pause before Osak continued speaking.

"...I want to let you know that I am coming home with Felicia. I will arrive exactly two weeks from today, and I will be staying for only one day. It will take me a whole day to arrive then I must leave on the night of day three to get back to America in the early hours of Day 4. So, I really have just a day and a half to stay before I must get back on a plane to return to America.

"It's okay, my son," said King Ebu. "Your impending presence here with us so we can do what we must do gladdens my heart. We will appreciate your presence here, even for just one hour. The reincarnation ceremony will last for 2 days then she needs a few days to heal from the circumcision. We can shorten the reincarnation ceremony,"

"It is not possible to stay beyond a day and a half, father," said Osak.

"Do you want to leave with her without waiting for the wound from the circumcision to heal?" King Ebu asked.

"It appears so. Yes, I will," said Osak.

"Okay then. If you feel okay with that, it's also good with me," said King Ebu. "I will start from tomorrow to put everything together from this end in anticipation of your arrival."

"Thank you father! I will see you soon."

Osak hung up, just as Bilky was about to say something.

"Is he coming with his white wife, did he say anything about that?" Bilky asked.

"I don't know, he hasn't mentioned anything about it to me."

"I am asking because he had once told me that the woman was against Uwa's circumcision. Maybe she has changed her mind," said Bilky. "If he had married from our community like we wanted him to, he wouldn't have had any issues with a wife like that, over a circumcision practice which has existed in our community since it was founded hundreds of years ago."

There were two things King Ebu needed to do right away to kick off the coming activities. The first was to call a meeting of the diviners and witch doctors in the community who would perform the reincarnation rituals and ceremony. The second was to make contact with a local circumciser. As Osak had given a firm date of his arrival, King Ebu felt comfortable now to notify the entire community about the coming rare event. This would be done through a town crier who would trek through the eight villages that made up the town to announce the King's invitation to the ritual. He would also direct a palace messenger to summon all the witch doctors in the community to the palace for a meeting.

The ritual itself was an exercise in esoteric craft by witch doctors, who would gather at a hilly spot in the center of the town where Uwa and Iken, the founders of the town, had first settled to cultivate the land and raised eight boys who went on to establish the villages that now constituted the community. The head witch doctor, while holding Felicia in his arms, would lead his colleagues in prayers and incantations. Libation would be poured on the spot and two cows would be slaughtered as offerings to the original first family. The ceremony would conclude with a grand feast, cultural dance and music, and other merriment at the king's palace.

The preparation that would put in place all of the components of such a huge ceremony was obviously going to be extensive, but King Ebu had been looking forward to that day. It would be expensive, too, but Osak had offered to fund the costs. He had conveyed the offer to King Ebu a week or so after he had firmly made up his mind to proceed with the ceremony, following Felicia's last bout with ill health.

***

It had been several weeks since Felicia's last episode with serious ill health. She was bubbly again, which made Osak think for a moment about aborting the plan, but he was not convinced that she won't get sick again. He had now bought into what his parents told him was the problem, and he was going to see it through to remove the supernatural hold on her. The plan's final stage of implementation therefore had to proceed.

Two weeks seemed to roll by quite fast during which Felicia's passport was delivered to him, and he had purchased round trip tickets to Africa for himself, Felicia and Zain, who was in the dark about the plan at this point. Osak did not want to take the chance of informing Zain about it, for fear she could leak the plan to Ingrid, whom Zain had grown very close to.

Zain admired Ingrid's kindness and simplicity and thought she was the perfect wife for her brother. She recalled being skeptical about her brother's idea to marry a white woman, when he had called and told her about it several years ago. She didn't think it would work because they were of different racial backgrounds. But in close to five months of knowing Ingrid, she came to the conclusion that she was a beautiful person inside and out. Osak had noticed this closeness over time and this had informed his decision not to inform Zain about what he planned to do until the very last minute. Osak did tell her about the convention in New York, that she would be going with him and Felicia, and that the primary reason for her coming was to care for Felicia during the four days they would be away. Zain thought it was odd that Ingrid was not going to the convention, but Ingrid explained she could use the four days of quiet time in the house to study for her examination. They would be in good hands in Osak, she had assured Zain. It all made sense to Zain, who looked forward to the trip. It would be her first trip to New York City.

They had taken off on a Friday morning for New York to the convention, so Zain thought. Ingrid had dropped them off earlier at the airport. The small commuter plane landed forty-five minutes later. Zain held Felicia in her arms. Osak led the way to a departure lounge/gate area where they sat on a long blue metal bench. There were hundreds of passengers at the departure gate and they were waiting to board an international flight. Minutes later, after Zain had made Felicia, who was asleep, comfortable in her stroller, Osak turned to Zain and revealed the bombshell.

"Zain," he called her name in a low voice to draw her attention. "We are going to Africa, to our country."

"What do you mean?" she asked. "I thought we were going to a convention of the hometown association here in New York."

"No, we are taking Felicia home for her reincarnation rite and circumcision."

Zain was speechless for several moments.

"You are Felicia's temporary mother right here

in this airport, as I process her departure with the airline counter and gate checkers before we board the plane."

"… Say you are her mother if you are asked any question about her," he told her.

"Does Ingrid know about this?" she asked.

"No, she does not. She wouldn't have agreed with it if I had told her about it."

Zain shook with fear and anxiety. It was true that their parents wanted the things Osak mentioned to be done to Felicia, and she had been in support, but since her arrival in America and her getting to know Ingrid very well, her opinion had begun to change. She could go along with the reincarnation rite which she thought Ingrid could be persuaded to go along with, but the circumcision part was now anachronistic in her evolved view about it. Her instinct right here and now sitting at the departure lounge listening to Osak was to refuse to go along with what he wanted to do.

"Do you plan to return to America?" she asked him, still incredulous.

"We will return, we will be away for only four days. I spoke with father a couple of weeks ago. They are preparing. We will be over there for just a day and a half."

"How will you explain Felicia's circumcision to Ingrid? Don't you know she will notice the excision?" She asked.

"Don't worry about that. I will deal with that whenever it comes up," he said to her.

"Remember to tell the agent that Felicia is your daughter if asked. Our flight should be boarding soon."

This was why Osak had brought her to America, so she could play this critical role in his plot.

The public address system came on to announce flights about to board passengers in the next five minutes, and the flight to West Africa was one of them. Everyone got up and proceeded to form a queue. Many stretched stiff legs after sitting for a long period of time. A female airport police officer, on routine patrol, walked into the gate area.

The officer appeared to have done so coincidentally. She noticed Felicia in her stroller and a dark skinned lady holding on to the stroller. That lady was Zain. Osak was in the queue just in front of Zain. The officer stopped by Felicia's stroller to banter with the lady and admire the beautiful baby in the stroller she thought was the lady's daughter.

"...Your daughter is very beautiful," said the officer. "How old is she?"

Zain was surprised at how direct the officer was. This was classic impromptu American interaction, a part of American culture Zain was not yet used to. She was thus confused about how to react to the police officer's compliment. She smiled at the officer and had no verbal response. The officer gazed at Felicia, smiling all the time as she did so. As a trained police officer, something clicked in her that made the situation suspicious.

Zain had appeared nervous when the officer had made her warm remarks about the baby. Zain had also not verbally acknowledged the compliments made about the baby. The baby had the facial characteristics of a Caucasian and she had long hair. Then as the officer walked away, she heard both Zain and the man in front of her she assumed to be Zain's husband speak briefly in a foreign language. The officer immediately suspected a potential child trafficking crime. Television news had featured a number of such cases in the country lately, and this contributed immensely to her suspicion.

Out of sight of the 'offending couple' she radioed headquarters about her suspicion. Osak and Zain moved up on the queue towards check in. Upon reaching the counter ten minutes or so after their encounter with the officer, they were approached by several police officers who asked them to step out of the queue for questioning.

Osak was calm, but Zain was nervous and it showed in her trembling.

"Let me see your identifications?" the lead officer, a white male, asked.

Osak handed over three passports and his driver's license to the officer who thoroughly checked through them. The officer faced Zain and asked whether she was the mother of the baby. Zain hesitated for several seconds before answering in the affirmative.

"Are you truly this baby's mother?" the officer asked again.

TO BE CONTINUED IN THE SEQUEL.